Quilted by Christmas

Other books in the Quilts of Love Series

Beyond the Storm
Carolyn Zane

A Wild Goose Chase Christmas
Jennifer AlLee

Path of Freedom
Jennifer Hudson Taylor

For Love of Eli
Loree Lough

Threads of Hope
Christa Allan

A Healing Heart
Angela Breidenbach

A Heartbeat Away
S. Dionne Moore

Pieces of the Heart
Bonnie S. Calhoun

Pattern for Romance
Carla Olson Gade

Raw Edges
Sandra D. Bricker

The Christmas Quilt
Vannetta Chapman

Aloha Rose
Lisa Carter

Tempest's Course
Lynette Sowell

Scraps of Evidence
Barbara Cameron

A Sky Without Stars
Linda S. Clare

Maybelle in Stitches
Joyce Magnin

A Stitch and a Prayer
Eva Gibson

A Promise in Pieces
Emily Wierenga

Rival Hearts
Tara Randel

A Grand Design
Amber Stockton

Hidden in the Stars
Robin Caroll

Swept Away
Laura V. Hilton & Cindy Loven

Masterpiece Marriage
Gina Welborn

A Stitch in Crime
Cathy Elliott

QUILTED BY CHRISTMAS

Quilts of Love Series

Jodie Bailey

Abingdon fiction™
a novel approach to faith

Nashville

Quilted by Christmas

ISBN-13: 978-1-4267-7361-7

Published by Abingdon Press, P.O. Box 801, Nashville, TN 37202

www.abingdonpress.com

Published in association with the MacGregor Literary Agency

Quilts of Love Macro Editor: Teri Wilhelms

Library of Congress Cataloging-in-Publication Data

Bailey, Jodie.
  Quilted by Christmas / Jodie Bailey.
    · pages ; cm. -- (Quilts of love series)
    ISBN 978-1-4267-7361-7 (softcover : acid-free paper) 1. Women teachers--Fiction. 2.
Grandmothers--Fiction. 3. Quilting--Fiction. 4. Christmas stories. I. Title.
  PS3602.A544Q55 2014
  813'.6--dc23

2014027914

Printed in the United States of America

1 2 3 4 5 6 7 8 9 10 / 19 18 17 16 15 14

To my grandmothers, Nanny and Bopum.
You taught me how to be patient,
how to love without conditions,
and how to face adversity while knowing
God is always there.
Without you, I have no idea who I'd be today.

Acknowledgments

No book is written in a vacuum, even though some days at the computer feel more solitary than others. Each time I write acknowledgments, I'm reminded once again how blessed I am to have the support of the people I love.

Paul, every day I realize again how blessed I am to be married to you. If I wrote you as a hero in a book, you would be unbelievable. Thank you for loving me and for giving me everything I need to pursue this dream and calling . . . and for making me coffee. I love you. More than you know and more every day.

Cailin, you are incredible. You are Mommy's treasure. I know you are going to be an awesome woman of God someday. I'm so proud of you!

Sandra Bishop, you believed in an Army wife in Georgia, writing a little ol' NASCAR story. You saw things in my writing that I didn't, and you've helped shape something I never saw coming . . . but God did. Thanks for being obedient to Him and for caring about me!

Ramona Richards, if you hadn't talked me off the ledge a few years ago and educated me in the fine line between "hero" and "stalker," who knows where I'd be today. Thank you for taking a chance on me!

Glenda Cook, when you walked into that book signing over twenty years after you told me I could be a writer, I knew how awesomely intricate and fascinating God's plan is. There is no way to tell how many students you've influenced and loved over the years, but I know one thing . . . this journey of mine would look a whole lot different without you in it. Thank you for being willing to still be a part.

Know what every writer needs? "Critter Sisters" like my Crit 13 ladies. Kimberly Buckner, Donna Moore, and Christina Nelson, though there are miles between us, we can't be separated. It's been up, it's been down, it's been all around, but we can still light up the country with prayer like a cell phone coverage map.

To Mom, for teaching me to see God in the little things.

To Dad, for being everything a girl could need . . . best friend, defender, shoulder to cry on . . . thank you.

To my students who truly are "my babies." To my "sister," Heather: God for sure put us together, and words can't express how grateful I am. Oh, and may He help "Mama" whenever we're in the same room. To Shalawn, who doesn't hesitate to tell me when she hears the voice of God and who keeps me going in the right direction. To "Mama" Dayton, who understood and who is truly a mama to every single one of her children, including me. And to the rest of my Freedom family, thank you!

And here's the part where I always forget someone. My Lesley, you're always there for me. I love you! Laura Ott, who knows the importance of good cookies, better phone calls, and child-free time. Dawn Lucowitz, the greatest cheerleader in the world. Donald and Shirley Melvin, who faithfully pray, probably even before I ask. JB and MM, who faithfully pray always. Culbreth Church, my second family. Jennifer McCarty, beta reader extraordinaire. Kristin Dudish, an Army wife and reader after my own heart. Eva Marie Everson, who first told me I needed the wisdom of Ramona Richards.

And to my Jesus . . . my everything. I'm awed You'd do that for me.

1

"4 . . . 3 . . . 2 . . . 1 . . ." The small crowd's voice rose in pitch and trembled with the chill as the lights flickered into life on the eighteen-foot tree in the small park in Hollings, North Carolina. Along Main Street, lampposts and white lights popped to life and bathed downtown in a warm glow.

Taryn McKenna shoved her hands deeper into the pockets of her coat to keep from blowing on her fingers again. All it did was make them colder. What global warming? It felt like every year the temperature dipped lower than the one before. The wind coming off the mountain tonight had a particular bite to it, like it had heard the same news as Taryn and wanted to make sure she felt it inside and out.

"Have you seen him yet?" Her younger cousin Rachel leaned close and did her best to whisper, though over the small crowd it seemed more like a shout.

Even Ethan, Rachel's recently adopted thirteen-month-old son, thought his mom's voice was too loud. He pressed four chubby fingers against her mouth with a wet, "Shh . . ."

For a minute, Taryn forgot she was supposed to be vigilant. She arched an eyebrow so high she could almost feel it touch the knit cap she wore over her shoulder-length dark hair. "It's pretty bad when the baby tells you to keep it down."

Rachel flicked honey-blonde hair over her shoulder and planted a smacky kiss on the little boy's cheek, eliciting a high-pitched squeal. "Come on, Mr. Manners. Let's go down to the fire station and see if we can find Daddy." She headed off to walk the three blocks out of downtown. "And we'll get Aunt Taryn out of the crowd before she can have an uncomfortable moment."

Taryn, who wasn't really Rachel's aunt even though her cousin had always called her that, shoved her hands deeper in her pockets and planted her feet. And after a comment like that, she should stay right here and let Rachel make the trek back to find her EMT fiancé all by herself. She looked over her shoulder toward her own house, two streets over from the park defining the center of Hollings. If she started walking now, she could have hot chocolate in hand and *It's a Wonderful Life* on the TV in under ten minutes.

Not as if she'd be hiding the way Rachel implied. She'd simply be warm and comfortable away from the crowd jostling her as they headed for the community center where the county's Christmas craft festival was cranking up.

The craft festival. She winced. "Rach?"

Several feet ahead of Taryn, her cousin miraculously heard her and turned around. "You coming?"

"I promised Jemma I'd come over and help with her craft booth." *Jemma.* The name was warm on her tongue. Born of the time her tiny toddler mouth couldn't quite get the *grandma* to work like it was supposed to. Her Jemma. The constant love in her life. As much as she wanted to go home and tuck in under a quilt, Taryn had promised, and she wouldn't let her grandmother down. "She's got some quilts she's selling in the community center."

Rachel's gaze bounced between the small brick building at the edge of the park and the fire station, invisible down the street and around the corner, where her fiancé probably waited for her to show up with his chicken and pastry dinner from the little church on, yes, Church Street. "I'll come with you and visit your grandmother for a second. I need to thank her for the cute little fireman quilt she made for Ethan's bed. I can't wait until he sees it on Christmas morning." She hefted her son higher on her hip without missing a step. "Mark is hoping the house will be ready by then so we can take Ethan over after he wakes up and have our first Christmas morning as a family in our own house, even if it's empty of everything but a tree."

"That's the single sappiest thing I've ever heard. And maybe the sweetest."

Ethan giggled like he knew exactly what Taryn had said.

Taryn knew better than to offer to take the boy for some snuggles of her own. This was all still new and joyful to Rachel. Give it a month. She'd be begging for a babysitter, and Taryn would be more than willing to oblige. The way her arms ached to snuggle the wiggling, giggling bundle told her so. She shoved the longing aside and slid sideways between two people. "Excuse me."

"Where did all of these people come from, anyway?" Rachel fell a half step behind her as the crowd thickened to funnel through the double doors into the community building.

"It's Christmas in the mountains, and it's tree lighting night. Half of them are tourists."

"Sure enough," said an older gentleman with a Boston accent. "Cold down here is a lot better than cold up north."

"Cold is cold." Taryn smiled into his kind face.

"But here, with all the evergreens and the rolling hills . . ." He breathed in deeply. "Feels like you ought to be able to catch Christmas in a bottle up here. Sell it maybe. It's like Christmas magic."

Okay, right. Because there was such a thing as Christmas magic. Where all your dreams came true. Taryn fought the urge to screw up her lips. Never going to happen. She scanned the crowd again, wanting to spot a familiar face and yet dreading it at the same time. It was miserable being torn in two by your own emotions.

"I know what you're thinking." Rachel was right on top of her, one hand holding Ethan's head to her shoulder protectively. "It will happen for you too. Who knows, maybe with what you heard tonight . . ." She wiggled her eyebrows.

Taryn knew her expression hardened, just from the way her jaw ached. "No. Don't start."

"You can't hide forever. Especially helping Jemma. If he's looking for you, this is the first place he'll go."

"If he was looking for me, he would have found me before tonight. Frankly, I told Jemma I'd help her before I knew he was in town, and had I known, I'd be home right now avoiding a scene." Maybe she should make an appearance, tell her grandmother she wasn't feeling well, and leave fast. It wouldn't be a lie. Her stomach was tying into deeper knots by the second. If she wasn't careful, the country-style steak Jemma had cooked for dinner might just make an encore appearance. "He won't look for me. He's home to see his family. And I'm not his family."

"You could've been if you hadn't been so stubborn." Rachel may have meant to mumble under her breath, but it came just as a lull in the crowd's conversation dropped, making it a loud and clear indictment.

Taryn stopped right in the flow of traffic just inside the door and turned to look Rachel hard in the eye. It was a mantra she'd stopped telling herself a long time ago, but hearing it now from her cousin, out loud for the first time, the words fired anger and released pent-up emotions Taryn thought she'd tamed long ago. "What did you just say?" The words bit through the air, hanging with icicles.

"Taryn . . ." Rachel's eyes widened like the eyes of a deer Taryn had once hit heading down the mountain into Boone. She looked just as frozen too. "I never should have spoken out loud."

"So it's okay to think it?" Was that how everyone saw Taryn? As the poor girl who let the love of her life get away? Waving a dismissive hand, Taryn turned and stalked off as best she could, leaving Rachel frozen in the crowd. Good. She deserved it. All those years she'd had Taryn's back, and now the truth came out. The whole mess was Taryn's fault, and even her cousin thought so.

By the time Taryn arrived at Jemma's tables, she was angry and over-stimulated. The crowd was too loud, the lights too bright, and the air too stuffy. More than anything, she wanted to pack a bag, hike up to Craven Gap, and pitch a tent for a week. She huffed into a spare metal folding chair and crossed her arms over her chest, garnering a warning glance from her grandmother, who was chatting with their preacher. Taryn sat up straighter and dropped her hands to her lap. She might be thirty, but Jemma still knew how to put her in her place.

Taryn let herself scan the room, filled with familiar townspeople and stranger tourists alike, but no jolt of adrenaline hit her at the sight of any of the faces. It disappointed and relieved her. Over the past dozen years, she'd managed to bury every emotion about those months deep down, so deep she hadn't realized how badly she wanted to see Justin Callahan.

Despite the longing, a conversation with him couldn't end well. Still, her eyes wouldn't stop searching, even though something told her she'd know if Justin walked in, whether she spotted him or not. From the time she was a child, her heart had always known when he was nearby.

Rachel stood on the far side of the room at Marnie Lewis's booth, which overflowed with all manner of jams and jellies. If she could, Taryn would slip over there and lay her head on Marnie's shoulder, unburdening herself of the tense anticipation knotted in her stomach. Where Jemma was all practicality, her best friend, Marnie, was the soft shoulder for Taryn's many tears. There had only been once when she'd had to refuse Marnie's comfort because the secret of those tears would have been too much for the older woman to bear.

But there was no time for pouring it all out now. Taryn shoved out of the rusting metal chair and busied herself straightening the quilts hanging from curtain rods hooked to a painted black peg board. Her fingers ran down the stitches of a red-and-white Celtic Twist, one of Jemma's latest creations. This one was done on the trusty Singer machine in the upstairs sewing room at the white house in the center of the apple orchard. Tourists loved Jemma's work, so she packed up the quilts she stitched by day and brought them to large craft fairs around Asheville and smaller ones in tiny valley towns like their own. The more tiny Hollings made its mark on the map as a North Carolina mountain tourist spot, the more out-of-towners discovered they had to have Jemma's work. Her Celtic designs practically walked out the door right by themselves.

Taryn ran her hands over a complicated Celtic Knot to smooth the wrinkles as a shadow fell over the fabric. "This one's a beauty, isn't it?" She angled her chin up, ready to put on her selling face to the latest tourist.

Instead, she met all too familiar hot chocolate brown eyes. His brown hair was shorter than she'd ever seen it, though the top seemed to be outpacing the sides in growth. His shoulders were broader under a heavy black Carhartt coat, his face more defined. Every muscle in her body froze even as her stomach jumped at the heat of seeing him. She'd known this day would come, knew he was in town now, but still, she wasn't ready.

Clearly, neither was he. He looked at her for a long moment, opened his mouth to speak, then was jostled by a tourist who stopped to peruse the lap quilts on the small plastic table. "This was a bad idea." Justin shook his head and, with a glance of what looked like regret, turned and blended into the crowd, leaving Taryn to watch him walk away. Again.

———

"What exactly was that all about?"

When Jemma offered Taryn a ride home as the craft show wound down for the evening, Taryn figured she was safe. After all, Jemma hadn't said one word about Justin's awkward appearance and rapid disappearance. Maybe she hadn't even noticed the entire exchange. In the bustle of answering questions and selling quilts, all she'd asked was if Taryn would come over tomorrow and spend part of her Saturday decorating the Christmas tree and working on Rachel's wedding quilt with her.

But now, as she pulled Taryn's kitchen door shut behind her, Jemma revealed just how much patience she had. About three hours' worth.

Taryn pulled two chunky diner-style coffee mugs down from the white wood cabinets and thunked them onto the ancient butcher block countertop. "What's all what about?" It was a long shot, but maybe the question had nothing to do with Justin at all. Maybe this was more about how she'd stalked into the booth and plopped into her chair like a three-year-old in full pout. Taryn rolled her eyes heavenward. *Please, God? I'm not ready to have the Justin conversation yet.*

"The little two-second exchange between you and a man who looked an awful lot like Justin Callahan all grown up."

Nope. It was exactly what Taryn had feared it was about. She yanked open another cabinet and dug out a plastic container of Russian tea. Every year, when the first breath of winter blew along the valley, Taryn mixed instant tea with dried lemonade, orange drink, and spices just like her mother always had. It kept her close, made Taryn feel like she could close her eyes and have her mother reappear whenever she needed her. Boy, did she ever need her tonight. "Want some tea?"

"It was him, wasn't it, Taryn?" The voice wasn't demanding, just gentle, maybe even a little bit concerned.

Demanding would have been better.

Taryn turned and leaned against the counter to find Jemma still by the back door, arms crossed over her red-and-green turtleneck sweater. "I asked you to come in for something warm to drink, not to answer questions I don't have answers to." She threw her hands out to the sides. "But yes, it was Justin. And why he came over to speak to me, I have no idea."

Jemma nodded, one gray curl falling out of place over her temple. "Looked to me like he wanted to talk to you and thought better of it once he looked you in the eye. Can't say I blame him. You looked scared to death."

Yeah. Because she didn't want him reading her mind and ferreting out all of her secrets. She might have done the right thing for him nearly twelve years ago, but it didn't mean he ever needed to know about it. "I was surprised."

"You always knew he'd come home someday. I'd have never thought it would take him this long. The army's kept him pretty busy, I'm guessing."

"He's been stationed overseas a lot. Too far to come home often. When he has been home, he's kept to Dalton on his side of the mountain. I'm pretty sure he hasn't been to Hollings since we were in high school." The minute the words left her mouth, Taryn wished she could pull a Superman and make the world spin backward just long enough to stop herself from saying them in the first place.

Jemma's eyebrow arched so high it was a wonder it didn't pop right off her forehead. "You kept track?"

"I'd run into his mom occasionally. Rarely. Every once in a while." Awkward encounters for Taryn because Ellen Callahan was always so friendly, so open, as though Taryn and her son hadn't flamed out in a screaming match in their front yard the night before he left for basic training. While she told Jemma almost everything, she'd kept those brief conversations a secret. The less they talked about Justin, the better, because talking about him kept her from pretending anything ever happened.

"I'll have some Russian tea." Jemma finally answered the long-asked question, then pulled a spoon from the drawer by the sink and passed it to Taryn. "You're going to have to talk to him sooner or later."

Taryn dug the spoon into the fall leaf-colored powder and dumped it into a mug. "I never plan to talk to him. At least not the way you're implying. And aren't you the one who told me for years that not talking to him was the better option?"

A car hummed by on the road in front of the house, loud in the sudden silence of the kitchen. Jemma didn't move, then she shook her head. "Opinions change. Maybe . . . Maybe I was wrong."

"No, you were exactly right. Besides, he's home for Christmas this year, and then he'll be back off to parts unknown in the world. If history is any indicator, he won't be back in Hollings for another dozen years, and by then . . ." She shrugged a *no big deal*. By then, she'd probably still be Taryn McKenna, schoolteacher, living in the small green house on School Street, except maybe she'd have half a dozen cats for company. It was what she deserved, and it was likely what she'd get.

With a long-suffering sigh, Jemma pushed herself away from the counter and ran light fingers down the back of Taryn's dark hair. "It's your choice, but I'll be praying."

Something in her tone froze Taryn's fingertip on the button for the microwave. "Why?"

Jemma let her touch drift from the crown of Taryn's head to the tips of her shoulder-length hair, just like she had when Taryn was a child, then planted a kiss on her granddaughter's temple. "Because I had a little chat with Marnie while you were taking down the booth tonight. You know how she knows everything about everybody."

"And you're nothing like her at all, are you, Jemma?" Taryn smiled in spite of the dread. If anyone knew the business of everybody on the mountain, it was her grandmother.

"Don't be cheeky, hon. Your mother and I taught you better."

The spoon clinked against the ceramic of the coffee mug as Taryn stirred her grandmother's tea, the spicy orange scent like a much-needed hug from her mother. The restlessness in her stomach settled. In a couple of weeks or so, Justin would be gone again, and she wouldn't have to worry about running into him, wouldn't have to worry about the split-in-half feeling of wanting to see him, yet wanting to hold him at a distance. "What did Marnie say?"

Jemma pulled Taryn close to her side and pressed her forehead to Taryn's temple. "Justin's not home for Christmas. He's out of the army. He's moved home to Dalton for good."

2

Taryn's arms ached. Her back ached. Even her fingers ached. How many boxes of Christmas decorations could Jemma hide in this attic? She blew an errant piece of hair out of her mouth, then reached up and tightened her ponytail. At least physical pain was preferable to thinking. She'd had more than enough time to think last night, since her brain stayed active long enough for her to know how the light in her bedroom shifted during every minute of the night.

One thing at a time. Focus on the here and now. In this moment, it was all about decorating Jemma's house for Christ-mas. They were already almost two weeks late, Jemma having decided to up her volunteer hours at the elementary school when she found out cuts in the art program were going to keep those precious children from making their traditional Christmas crafts.

With a huff, Taryn hefted yet another plastic container and hauled it to the door, feeling carefully for the narrow attic stairs leading to the second floor. "Only one more after this." She passed the box to Jemma and turned for one last trip.

"You should have let me help you."

"Really?" Taryn turned on the stairs to look down at her grandmother, who stood waiting next to several shoulder-high stacks of boxes in the hallway. "Because you falling down the stairs trying to carry those things last year didn't give me enough of a heart attack."

Jemma brushed the words away. "It was a sprained ankle. You act like I broke every bone in my body and cracked my head to boot."

"You're like a cat, Jem." Taryn pulled herself up the stairs and called over her shoulder, "How many of those nine lives have you used?"

"Twelve?"

Taryn sniffed a short laugh. It was probably true. Her grandmother refused to accept the fact seventy was in the rearview mirror and eighty was coming up fast. The woman was forever young, although she sometimes overestimated her abilities. At the rate she was going, Jemma was going to live forever, sewing and volunteering until Jesus cracked the sky and took everybody home.

She had to.

Taryn grabbed the last container and dragged it to the stairs, then stopped to look out the window facing the orchards. For generations, the Brodigans had worked the huge apple trees that rolled away toward the mountains outside of Hollings. After Taryn's grandfather died from a lightning bolt of an aneurysm in his brain thirteen years ago, Jemma leased the trees out to a national company. Now, Brodigan apples were blended into apple sauce, juice, and pie filling all over the country, and Jemma made a nice little sum from the lease every year, enough to allow her to volunteer and to quilt her hours away without worrying about how the bills would get paid.

Today, the dark sky over the orchard fired pellets that smashed white against the window, rapidly obscuring the view of the trees. "It's sleeting."

"Is it?"

"Yep. It's coming down pretty hard too." It was a good thing Taryn kept clothes in her old bedroom here. Even though it was only five miles back to her house in town, weather like this could make the mountain roads treacherous. "It's sticking to the window pretty good."

"Sleet doesn't stick. It bounces."

"Well, this sure isn't snow. It's too pellety."

"Is *pellety* even a word, Miss High School Teacher?" Jemma's quiet laugh floated up the stairs. "If it's little pellets and it's smushing against the window, it's not sleet. It's graupel."

What? "Now who's making up words? Is *graupel* even a real thing, or did you read it in *Alice in Wonderland,* because it sounds like something Lewis Carroll would make up."

"It's as real as you and me. I read about it on the Wikipedia."

Taryn rolled her eyes up and nodded at the ceiling. Jemma and her laptop. Buying her the machine last year for Christmas was either crazy smart or crazy insane. Jemma had way too much knowledge about the trivial now and even had a favorite online hobby, following the British royal family on Twitter. "You can't believe everything you read on Wikipedia."

"I verified it with a Web search, just like you taught me. And that graupel won't be too much of a problem. Usually doesn't accumulate to an inch."

Taryn nodded again, unable to argue against the combined knowledge of Jemma and Google. "Well, there you have it. Good to know." She cast one more glance around the large attic to make sure the box by the stairs was the last one. As she turned to leave, the sun broke through the snow-heavy clouds and streamed onto the unfinished wood floor, catching the reflection of something shiny behind where the Christmas boxes had been stacked. As curious as a cat in her own right, Taryn couldn't resist. She crossed the attic and knelt down to knee walk into the eaves, near where the rafters met the frame of the house. A small square steamer trunk was wedged as far back as it could get in the space. She pulled it out, dragging it along the floor and scraping her knuckles against the exposed rafters.

"What are you doing up there?" Jemma's voice came again, laced with impatience this time. "I'm ready to get this decorating party started."

"Shiny things, Jemma. I'll be down in a minute."

"Don't get lost up there. I'm going to go warm up some soup for lunch, then we can decide which tree goes where." It would be a chore in itself, since Jemma owned enough trees to put one in every room of the house.

"Okay." Taryn hardly paid her grandmother any attention. She'd explored this attic from top to bottom as a child and later as a teenager. This box was one she'd never seen before. It didn't look as old as half of the trunks up here, the ones dating back to when her great-great-great-grandfather built the house, and that made it doubly intriguing.

The latches popped easily, and the trunk swung open without a squeak, releasing the sweet scent of fabric and thread, evoking immediate images of Taryn's long afternoons curled up in the glider rocker reading, while Jemma pieced quilts in the sewing room downstairs. Taryn closed her eyes and relished the warm memory for a moment before peeking into the trunk.

A quilt. Well, to be more exact, the beginnings of a quilt. Cut and pieced for the most part, only a few squares were unfinished. A nine-patch, green and cream. And something about it looked familiar. On a hunch, Taryn laid out the mixed green-and-cream squares, alternating them with solid cream squares until a small nine-by-nine block formed. An Irish chain. She looked closer. Hand-stitched. Jemma never made Irish chains because they were the traditional wedding quilt for the McKennas, Taryn's father's side of the family. The quilt Grandma McKenna had pieced for Taryn's mother hung on the wall in Taryn's office at home, the symbol of what an unwanted child could do to a marriage, a silent reminder she'd done the right thing.

Taryn lifted a quilt piece and rubbed it against her cheek, willing herself not to cry at the sneak attack tears. *Focus on the here and now.*

Taryn rocked back on her heels. The fabric was pristine, slightly rough in her hands and relatively new. Jemma only knew two McKennas of marriageable age, herself and Rachel. The only one of the two of them who had ever even come close to needing a quilt was Rachel, and hers was partially stitched and patiently waiting in Jemma's sewing room. It was certain Taryn had no prospects.

Interesting. The only McKenna Irish chain Jemma had ever pieced was Rachel's, and she'd only started it recently. This one had no one to claim it.

"Taryn?" Jemma's step sounded on the stairs.

Feeling inexplicably guilty, like she'd peeked into Jemma's private journal, Taryn crammed the pieces back into the trunk, latched it, and shoved it out of the way just as her grandmother appeared at the top of the stairs. "Did you find anything interesting?"

"No." Taryn stood, swiping dust from her jeans, and brushed past her grandmother, pulling the last remaining Christmas box up to chest height and heading down the stairs. Whatever it was, now didn't feel like the right time to ask questions. "Nothing that can't wait until another time."

"And then, the stinking dog took off with his steak anyway."

Jemma had told the story to Taryn a dozen different times, every single time they put up the Christmas decorations in the old house. And every time, both of them laughed just as hard.

"I'd love to have seen the look on Grampa's face." Taryn hung a purple ball on the tree in the sewing room and stepped back to make sure it had filled the small hole in the decorations. Fact was, Taryn didn't need to see the look on her grandfather's face. She could picture it just fine. Sometimes, it felt like he'd been gone only a few days instead of nearly half of her life.

With an amused sigh, Jemma swiped at the corner of her eye. "He was something else, wasn't he?"

"Yes, he was. Just like you."

Jemma waved a dismissive hand and reached up to tweak the silver bow she'd tied to the top of the tree. "There. Now this one's done, and we can move to the one in my bedroom."

The old glider rocker creaked as Taryn dropped into it, the exertion of the day already exhausting her. "You're going to put a tree in every room?"

"Sweetie, we are just getting started. Wait 'til you see what I've got for the outside of the house this year. It'll look like a fairyland when we're done."

Nobody did Christmas like Jemma did Christmas. She could open up the house and sell tickets to tourists the same way she sold her quilts.

Quilts. With all of the flurry of decorating, Taryn had nearly forgotten the hand-sewn green-and-white Irish chain in the attic. It had to be special. Although tourist quilts were sewn by machine, personal quilts were a whole other thing entirely. Jemma stitched quilts for family by hand, and the tight stitches told the story. Even at seventy-three, Taryn's grandmother had steady hands and keen eyesight. Her current project was the blue-and-white Irish chain quilt for Rachel's wedding, one she'd been steadily sewing by hand for several weeks. The quilt took most of her free time.

And a ton of patience. It would drive Taryn positively batty to sit still as long as it took to stitch a quilt. She'd helped several times, but to do one all by herself? Jemma knew better than to even suggest it.

"Jemma?"

"Hm?" Her grandmother reached up to fluff the bow again, turning it to catch the light in a different way. "Does this look better?"

"Yes." Drawing her feet underneath her, Taryn rocked the chair gently back and forth. She could come out and ask what the quilt was for, but something stopped her. If Jemma went to the trouble of hiding it, there was a reason. Asking outright would slam Jemma shut tighter than an apple blossom bud in cold weather. "Tell me about the McKenna quilts."

Jemma's hand hesitated, then she smoothed the ribbons of the bow down the tree, fluffing them at strategic points. "What's got you asking about them now?"

"Because you're sewing one for Rachel, and she's not even your granddaughter."

"Jealous?" A teasing lilt took the sting from the question.

"Not at all." Long ago, Taryn had chosen the single life, deciding it was best for her. She'd never looked back.

Taking a step away from the tree, Jemma set her hands on her hips. "Think it's done?"

"I think it's beautiful." As always. Jemma fussed and fidgeted until everything was exactly the way she wanted it. As a result, everything she did was exact and perfect in a way Taryn envied. With a satisfied nod, Jemma settled herself into the chair in front of her sewing machine. "Rachel reminds me so much of you."

"I know." Taryn was fourteen when her mother, Jemma's daughter, died of liver cancer that crept up and stole her almost before anyone knew what was happening. The next winter, a patch of ice between Hollings and Asheville robbed Rachel of her mother. The dual loss had bonded the girls, though Taryn's father grew even more hostile in the grief of losing his sister.

The difference was, Rachel was marrying her lifelong sweetheart while Taryn had pushed hers away. Rachel and Mark had danced the relationship dance since he moved to Hollings with his dad in the fourth grade. Everyone in town knew they'd get married someday, even though the two of them got together and broke up dozens of times . . . until it stuck for good right out of college. Heavy rains had pushed back the completion date of their house on the other side of the mountain, forcing a two-month delay in the wedding as well, but after five years of dating, the big event was scheduled for New Year's Eve, just a handful of weeks away.

And they had already adopted a child. Well, Rachel had. Mark's part would be formal as soon as they were married. Something like this could happen only to Rachel. When Ethan's addict mother came to Rachel, who worked as a crisis counselor in nearby Asheville, God had led Mark and her to a quick decision, almost before they started praying. Ethan was theirs. Somehow, they'd known it from the first instant they saw him. He just became available a couple of months before they were officially ready. For now, he lived with Rachel at her parents' house, one set of grandparents about to be doubly lonely when their daughter set up her own house in a few weeks.

Taryn tried not to acknowledge any jealousy.

Jemma clucked her tongue, drawing Taryn back into the conversation. "Both of you so young to lose so much."

"So why make the quilt?"

"You've heard this story before."

"Humor me." Taryn was looking for clues, unable to fight back the notion she should keep quiet about her attic find. "Tell me the story."

"It's been a tradition for as far back as anyone knows for the McKenna women to make quilts for their children when they marry. Boy or girl, they get those quilts on their wedding day. Hand-sewn." Jemma reached over to her sewing table and lifted the edge of the partially finished quilt, heaped in a riot of blue and white. "With your Gramma McKenna and Rachel's mother both gone, there's no McKenna woman to sew one for Rachel." She seemed lost in the fabric. "I can't bear for her not to have a quilt for her wedding day. She'll be thinking of it. I know. So I'm filling in. But it's a secret." Jemma stood and swiped at invisible lint on her pants. "And don't you tell her. If she knew, she'd want to help, and the bride can't help sew her own quilt. Your Gramma McKenna told me all about it. There's a lot of rules with this particular tradition. Like it absolutely has to be an Irish chain. Nothing else."

Now they were coming to information Taryn needed. She dropped her feet to the floor and sat forward in the chair. "Why?"

"The McKennas can trace their roots all the way back to Ireland. So many legends about them. Makes the Brodigan in me jealous." Jemma flashed a grin and straightened a stray ornament. "They're proud of it. When Rachel's mother died and your Gramma McKenna knew she didn't have too much longer herself, she sat me down and let me in on the entire story. And I've told you before too."

"But I never get tired of hearing it." It was true, even if it wasn't exactly true at the moment.

"We Irish love a good story, don't we?" Tilting her head, Jemma studied the bow on the tree. "You're taller than I am. Come and straighten this so it hangs right."

Taryn obeyed, knowing Jemma would get back to her tale soon enough.

"The long and short of it is each wedding makes a new link in the chain, sort of like other families would have a new branch in the family tree. When the McKennas came over from Ireland, they chose the simple chain pattern to represent the family and how it would continue on even in a new country. Beautiful story." She nodded as Taryn tipped the bow to the left. "Perfect. Now let's go finish the other tree."

Following the pint-sized whirlwind that was her grandmother, Taryn couldn't help feeling there was more to the story, more than she'd heard before. If the Irish chain was a McKenna tradition, why did her Brodigan grandmother have an unfinished quilt in her attic?

3

Here." Jemma dropped a bundle of fabric into Taryn's lap as she passed and settled herself into the glider rocker near the fireplace. "All we need to do is go out to the back of the orchard to get the live tree for the den here, and we'll be finished. I can't wait for the house to smell like Christmas as much as it looks like Christmas." Breathing in deeply, Jemma smiled at the room. "So far, the rest of the house looks wonderful. Thanks for your help."

Taryn glanced around the small den as she unrolled the cloth in her lap. The tiny room couldn't compete with the larger, airier living room at the front of the house, but Jemma loved the den, its stone fireplace dominating the space, hardwood floors gleaming, white walls reflecting the multicolored lights strung through the evergreens hanging from the mantel.

The rough-hewn mantel dripped with lights, while Mary and Joseph and the shepherds waited patiently above for baby Jesus to make an appearance. "I only did it because I knew you were making gingersnaps today. I'm expecting a container of them before I leave." Pushing deeper into the leather recliner by the door to the kitchen, Taryn ran a finger along the blue- and-white fabric in her hands. "And what would you like me to do with this?" She knew, but her distaste for sewing was legendary, and there was nothing more fun than needling Jemma.

Jemma's chair rocked gently as her needle flashed through her own blue-and-white stack almost as fast as any sewing machine. That took practice beyond Taryn's years or patience. She smiled but otherwise ignored Taryn's teasing. "It's Rachel's quilt. If I'm going to get it pieced before the wedding, you're going to have to help me." She tossed a spool of white thread to Taryn without missing a beat in her rocking.

Rachel. Taryn licked the end of the thread and aimed it through the needle Jemma had stuck in the center of her fabric. At some point, Taryn would have to choke down her pride and have a conversation with her cousin. Rachel had only said what everyone who knew Justin and Taryn thought, what she'd thought herself many times. Stalking away had been childish. Warranted maybe, but childish nonetheless.

And then there was Justin. Catching the tip of her tongue between her teeth, Taryn joined two strips of fabric and started stitching a blue-and-white nine patch. Sewing left too much time to think. What she needed was a good, body-pushing, muscle-grinding hike up Brown Mountain. Then she wouldn't be able to think about anything except pacing her breath and watching her step. Any thoughts about missing Justin after his brief reappearance would be forced to the side of the trail.

"Why don't you just talk to him?" Jemma glanced at her watch and went back to her task.

"I'm sorry? Talk to who?" Taryn knew who, and it scared her a little. For as long as she could remember, Jemma had this uncanny ability to read her mind, like she could reach in and pull out the thoughts whenever she wanted. It was by no means supernatural. With Jemma, it was all about knowing how to read her granddaughter. It didn't make the occurrences any less creepy. At some point, Taryn had to develop a poker face to keep her thoughts away from her grandmother's too astute observations.

"You know very well who. And you need to be talking while you sew. I'm behind on this quilt. The wedding's coming up faster than we think, and there's Christmas baking in the middle."

At some point, Jemma was going to have to give up the hand-stitching and move on to sewing machines for family quilts, but it didn't look like the time would be today. With a sigh that started somewhere around her toes, Taryn went back to stitching, slower than Jemma, but quick enough to appease her.

Why didn't she just talk to him? The fire popped, and a log shifted in a firework of sparks before Taryn answered. "Because it's awkward. Too much time has passed. I mean, he's practically a stranger at this point, even though there was a time I kind of thought . . ." This was the hard part. "One day we'd get married—do the whole have a kid thing . . ." The needle nearly caught the end of her thumb. She'd better slow down, or Rachel would have bloodstains on her wedding quilt. An errant hair tickled her nose, and she blew hair out of her mouth. "And it didn't happen."

"You protected his future at the cost of your own. Is it possible you resent him because of it?"

This was the most Jemma had talked about Justin in more than a decade, though she'd held Taryn's hand and supported her when the world cracked apart. It was like breaking open the seal on King Tut's tomb. Taryn's cheeks flared hotter than the fire crackling in the stone fireplace. "I don't resent him. What I did was the right thing." She'd learned from her father's example and saved all of them from a heap of trouble, even though it hurt.

The only sounds in the room were the tick of the Regulator wall clock in the kitchen and the crack of the fire. Jemma silently glided her rocker back and forth so long, it gave Taryn hope the conversation was over.

But then, her grandmother spoke. "Maybe I've kept quiet too long."

"What do you mean?"

Before Jemma could answer, the sound of an engine glided close. Taryn sat up and laid her quilt pieces on the arm of the recliner. The house sat half a mile off the road, almost hidden by the orchard. Accidental drive-bys simply didn't happen. "Are you expecting company?" True to Jemma's Wikipedia research, the graupel had stopped almost as quickly as it started, leaving the roads clear, but it was still too cold for most of Jemma's septuagenarian buddies to venture out this afternoon. Besides, most of them knew it was decorating day, and there would be far too much activity for Jemma to be interrupted.

Jemma glanced at her watch with a slight nod. "Sure am. I decided last year climbing on the roof to hang tree lights is for the birds. Hired me somebody to do it this year." She slipped her feet into her tennis shoes and stood, setting aside her sewing in the vacated chair.

"Jack Truewell's older than you are, Jem. He has no more business being on the roof than you do. I'd have done it for you." Jack had been the go-to handyman around Hollings since before Taryn was born. It was well known he'd fix anything, would do anything for a few bucks or a few jars of homemade apple butter. Still, the man was getting up there. Sooner or later he'd have to retire, if for no other reason than to keep Taryn from worrying herself into an ulcer over the possibility he'd slide off the roof and break his hip.

"Jack Truewell got married last week. He's honeymooning in Punta Cana in the Dominican Republic."

"Do what?" Now this was news worth talking about. "To who?"

Jemma flashed a grin as she passed Taryn's chair on her way to the kitchen and the back door. "Emma Westin. Surprised everybody. Went down to the justice of the peace at the courthouse in Asheville, got married, and hauled outta here before anyone even realized they were sweet on each other."

"Well, wonders never cease." It was one of Jemma's favorite expressions, and Taryn lobbed it out there now. Jack Truewell and the owner of the only beauty shop in Hollings, where all of the women of Jemma's generation went to get their hair set on Friday so they'd look good for church on Sunday. Aqua Net and rollers ruled Emma's world. And she was easily ten years Jack's junior. Taryn grinned. Good for both of them. "So who'd you call if Jack's gone?"

The weather stripping on the back door popped as Jemma pulled the door open.

"Afternoon, Jemma." The deep voice wafted through the laundry room, across the kitchen, and into the den where it rested on Taryn's ears like a heavy blanket, almost suffocating her in shock.

Justin. Jemma had hired Justin.

Just what did she think she was up to?

———

This must be what a panic attack felt like. Or a heart attack. Taryn laid a hand on her chest and tried to press her thumping heart back into place. Dropping into the bentwood rocker in Jemma's upstairs sewing room, she laid her head back and stared at the ceiling. Stupid. This was all stupid. It was just Justin. Her best friend growing up. The guy she dated for two years in high school.

The man she thought she'd grow up to marry.

The man whose baby she'd put up for adoption without telling him.

She groaned and dropped her head between her knees, rocking chair creaking at the movement. This was the mountain she had to climb.

It was the right thing to do at the time. He was in basic training, embarking on the career he'd dreamed of all of his life. She was headed to college, bruised by their breakup during a fight driven by her neediness and his truthfulness.

He needed to go. She'd stood right by him until it was time, then begged him not to leave, even tried to manipulate him into staying. It was a brutal good-bye because of her impatience and neediness. What should have been a temporary good-bye wound up lasting more than a decade.

Because she'd listened to her father.

Taryn closed her eyes against the sight of him storming out the back door of Jemma's house, where Taryn had lived since her mother's death, craving the love missing from her house with her mother gone.

She'd had her hands in dishwater, cleaning up after dinner while Jemma was at her women's group meeting at church. Head reeling from the appearance of two pink lines on a pregnancy test, Taryn found the dishwater warm and soothing. She couldn't call Justin in basic at Fort Benning, and there was no way he would call her, not after the things she'd said and done. She'd have to call his parents later and see if they'd be willing to give up the address. It was certainly not the way she'd choose to tell him, and as bubbles popped against her hands, she prayed he wouldn't think she'd done this on purpose to bring him back.

When her father stepped through the back door, it had capped a day already fraught with emotion. She hadn't seen him in months. When she moved to Jemma's, he made himself even scarcer than in the fourteen years before. His wife was gone, and he viewed her death as a release from all obligations. He was content to live the carefree life he'd always resented Taryn for stealing from him, the life he'd always felt her mother had denied him when she got pregnant at eighteen.

Just like Taryn.

Taryn dried her hands and forced herself to face him. He smelled of the sticky sweet tar from his day of work with the road commission, while dust and asphalt caked his neon yellow shirt. He had a white plastic grocery bag in hand. "Know you're heading out to Pennsylvania tomorrow for college." He dropped the bag with a clatter on the counter. "Thought I'd at least come tell you good-bye. Bring you some pens and stuff to use at school."

It was the nicest thing Taryn could ever remember him doing. It figured. Just as she was leaving town to move seven hours away, he decided to do a dad thing. Just as she figured out she was about to become a parent herself, he stepped up to the plate and kicked a little of the dirt off his shoes.

What would have happened if he hadn't settled his bag on the counter right next to the empty pregnancy test box? If his face hadn't reddened under the weathered skin and his eyes hadn't hardened like the same roads he slaved over every day? He'd snatched the box up, stalked across the small kitchen, and nearly backed her against the counter, shoving the white- and-pink indictment into her face with such speed the thin cardboard tweaked her nose.

"Are you pregnant?" The words were so quiet, they could hardly be called a whisper, but they were so much worse than any shout. So much worse.

Taryn didn't have to answer. She knew the truth was all over the fear in her face.

"It's the Callahan boy's baby, isn't it?" His voice dropped deeper as the box shook between them, blurred by its closeness and wreaking havoc on eyes already hot with unshed tears. "You will not ruin his life." The words vibrated. "He has a future ahead of him, and you will not ruin his life the way you and your careless mother ruined mine. You will not tie him to you by getting pregnant." His eyes were granite. "Do you hear me?" The final shout pounded hard against her ears, leaving them ringing, stinging almost as badly as the sheer contempt in his eyes. "You're just like her. I should've known the apple wouldn't fall far from the tree." With a bitter chuckle at his own irony, he threw the box at her feet, grabbed the bag from the counter, and stalked out the back door, slamming it so hard behind him the

Franciscan dogwood plate Taryn had just washed slipped from the edge of the counter and shattered on the floor.

Taryn pressed her hands hard against her eyes, sagging hard against the counter. The decision had solidified then. She would not, could not, trap Justin the way her mother had trapped her father. Couldn't stand to see his eyes fill with bitterness toward her, toward their child, the way her father's had always looked at her. She would not wreck his dreams.

So she scuttled her own instead. The only way to keep Justin from finding out was to keep everyone else in Hollings from finding out. It was so old-fashioned, so 1930, the way she ran off to the University of Pennsylvania as planned and refused to come home for the entire first year, until the baby was born in May. She never held her baby girl. The decision still gutted her. She should have, just once.

A few times a year, she heard from Sarah or from her adoptive parents. Short notes. School pictures. Although Taryn had wanted a fully closed adoption, all parties anonymous to one another, Sarah's adoptive parents had pleaded for an open one so Sarah could know her history, have a connection to her roots. It had been a reluctant agreement, but as the years passed, Taryn found herself looking forward to those letters more and more, though she'd long ago silenced any requests from the parents to come and visit. If Sarah wanted to see her birth family, she'd ask herself, unprompted.

In her grief after the baby's birth, Taryn had needed her grandmother, someone to let her know she was loved, even though she'd all but abandoned her own child. She moved closer to home to UNC-Asheville and decided to be a teacher.

Oh, the irony, the absolute unfathomable mind of God, that Taryn McKenna taught history to high schoolers and stood in front of them as a role model.

Footsteps stomped across the roof, bringing her back to Jemma's sewing room, the gently swaying rocking chair, and the mildly sweet smell that would always be uniquely Jemma in her memory, of fabric and thread and the faint hint of sewing machine oil.

Now here was Justin, clomping around on Jemma's roof twelve years later, after looking her in the eye and turning away less than twenty-four hours before. Yeah, this day was coming, but did it have to be today?

Her grandmother had some 'splaining to do about what exactly she thought she was up to bringing him here. Jemma had grieved over the adoption and the secrecy right along with Taryn, but having been seated in the front row for her daughter's marriage to Taryn's father, the course of action had been clear to her just as it had been to her granddaughter. In fact, she'd encouraged it.

Speaking of Jemma, it was time to have her answer a few questions. Taryn pressed her hands to her knees and stood as the footsteps stopped directly over her head, followed by a thump and repeated vague scrapings. Yeah, now was as good a time as any to go anywhere else but here.

Problem was, Jemma was nowhere in the house. A quick peek out the back door in the laundry room showed the old gray Chevy Blazer stood in its usual place under the pecan tree at the corner of the house, but Jemma seemed to have vanished from the planet.

So she was avoiding an inevitable conversation with her granddaughter. Or she'd hopped up on the roof after all, helping Justin for all she was worth. Either way, she was in trouble.

Taryn was halfway across the kitchen when two sharp raps sounded at the back door and the hinges squeaked. "Hey, Jemma? We've got a problem."

Taryn whipped around, trapped in plain sight in front of the man from whom she was trying to hide.

Justin's brown eyes widened at the sight of her in the kitchen, his eyebrows shooting up toward his hairline. His hair was closer cropped than the floppy look he'd worn in high school. Twelve years hadn't dulled the brown in it.

She shouldn't be noticing.

"Hey." His greeting was hesitant, but he stepped through the door and into the mudroom, eyes still on her. This Justin was different, leaner, his work jacket tight over broad shoulders tapering to a lean waist. The army had been good to Justin Callahan. "I was wondering if that was your car out in the driveway."

"Yeah."

"It's practical. Good for snowy roads around here and all." Justin leaned a hip against the washing machine by the door and nodded his approval.

Taryn crossed her arms over her chest and tried to hold herself together. What exactly was going on here? The last time she'd talked to him, it had been a shouting match that brought his parents out of the house to try to intervene. Now he wanted their first conversation to be about the practicality of her vehicle?

Before she could ask him what he needed, he shifted and looked away from her, out the window on the back door. "It sure is a far cry from Fred, though."

Fred. Just the sound of the name unraveled some of the tension in her shoulders and tugged at the corner of her lips. She stuck her hands in the pockets of her jeans. "Fred was one of a kind."

Justin grinned. "Now Fred, he was a truck. The truck. To end all trucks."

Fred was an old, beat-up 1986 Ford pickup, the truck her grandfather had driven all over the orchard from Taryn's toddlerhood up until the day he died. There hadn't been a need for Jemma to call anyone to dinner in this house. The sound of Fred bouncing and rattling up the small road through the middle of the orchard was enough to let everyone know Grampa was home and dinner ought to be on the table. When Taryn's grandfather died, the old truck was relegated to the back barn for several months, until Taryn's heart ached for the abandoned vehicle in need of someone to love it. Her wounded daughter heart couldn't stand the thought of anything, even a truck, without someone to care for it. She'd found the keys and, with Justin's help, got the truck polished and running again.

Justin broke her memories. "We rattled all over this mountain in Fred senior year."

"Cassette deck blaring."

"Bouncing in time to Nitty Gritty Dirt Band singing . . ."

"'Fishin' in the Dark.'" Taryn finished in harmony with him. In spite of everything that had happened in the meantime, the memory she hadn't allowed herself to take out and play with warmed her.

She wasn't ready for warmth. It had been too long.

"So, what ever happened to Fred?"

"I sold him." In a fit of knowing too much, the same day she'd faced her father, Taryn had needed to do something drastic, to cut away something as punishment for what she'd done. "Sold him to Bob O'Sullivan the day before I left for college. He'd had his eye on Fred for a long time." She crossed her arms again, building a barrier between them. "So, what's the problem you needed to talk to Jemma about? Was she not up on the roof with you?"

His smile slipped, his expression moving to one she recognized from marching band in high school. All business. "Haven't seen her. Her Blazer's in the driveway though."

"Maybe she's out in the barn." Taryn took two steps toward the door, then hesitated. To go out would mean to brush past Justin, and the last time she'd touched him, there had been a world of trouble to pay, at least for her.

Glancing at his watch, Justin jerked his head toward the door. "I've got to be somewhere in half an hour. Got to look at the Duncans' fence around the back of their orchard. I'll show you, then you can fill Jemma in. Get your coat. I'll meet you outside. Ladder's around by your old window."

Of course it was. Where else would it be?

4

The wind was kicking up pretty hard by the time Taryn found Justin on the back side of the house, sitting with his legs dangling into space over the window of Jemma's sewing room. To the southwest, clouds piled on top of one another, angry and dark. They might have had Jemma's graupel earlier, but Taryn had smelled wind like this before and watched clouds like those. It was not snow building this time.

Justin slid back on the shingles and stood, brushing off his pants. "There's a nasty mess of rain headed our way. Temperature's gone up about twenty degrees since this morning."

They'd talked about cars. Why not throw the weather in there too? Seemed like a right and natural progression. "Yeah. Rain." If she could do it without him seeing, Taryn would plant a palm right in the middle of her forehead. Around him, her brain jumbled, past folding onto present, truth intertwining with secrets.

Justin looked at her, cocking his head to one side before he grinned. "I missed you, Tar." Without pausing to let her react, he slapped his hands against his thighs. "Okay, let me show you what I found." He knelt about three feet back from the edge of the roof and motioned for her to join him.

He missed her? She had to have heard him the wrong way. Taryn shoved her hands into her pockets and dug her fingers into her thighs. How could he even look at her without thinking about how she'd tried to manipulate him into giving up all of his dreams? How she'd used everything in her power to get him to go back on a promise made to one another—and to God—long before they ever started dating?

Justin was blessed he wasn't privy to her screaming internal questions. "I came up to hang Jemma's lights, but when I got over here, the wood beneath the shingles felt soft, so I checked." He peeled back a few shingles. The wood he exposed was dark and damp and swollen, almost the consistency of thick wheat bread. "She's got a major leak here. Much more and she'll have a nice sunroof in her sewing room."

All other thoughts fled. Damage like this could mean tricky emergency repairs, even if it hadn't spread from this one point. "Why hasn't it spotted the ceiling yet?"

Justin shrugged. "I have no idea. It should have, because this is mighty damp." He poked at the soft wood. "This part of the roof goes straight through to the rooms beneath, so the water has to be going somewhere. There's no attic over this section of the house because it juts out, probably an addition made after the original house was built."

Taryn knelt beside Justin and poked a finger at the soft wood. "My great-grandfather. He had more kids than the previous generations." Children. She could not think about children around him. Some heavy-duty vibes probably shot off her every time she did.

"Well," Justin dropped the shingles back into place. "I took a look around the rest of the roof while I had a few minutes. She's got a few more soft spots. Not as bad as this one, but the house needs a new roof. The sooner the better. The actual reroofing can wait until spring, but there will be some serious problems if she doesn't jump on some of these patches quickly." He stood and reached down a hand to help her up, though she acted like she didn't notice. "Call around. Get some estimates. I'll throw one in if you want. Go with who'll do the work the best for the least amount of money, and if we get a good stretch of weather, get it done fast." He glanced at the sky. "Until then, I'll run over to Dad's house and get a tarp to put up here and cover this before we get dumped on."

"Jemma's got some tarps in the barn." Taryn pinched the bridge of her nose and muttered, "And it sounds like we've already been dumped on."

"I'm sorry."

"Don't be. You didn't Swiss cheese the roof."

"Sarcasm. Some things never change, do they?" He bent and retrieved a hammer near the edge of the roof. "That was always one of the best things about you. I'd almost forgotten." He swept his arm toward the ladder and waited for her to step in front of him.

Instead, she stood firm, gripped by the sudden need to keep him talking. For a few minutes, talking about something as mundane as roof repair, it had felt like she was young again, like she'd never pushed him away with her seriously screwed-up behavior. "So why was it a mistake to come by Jemma's booth at the craft fair and see me last night?" Taryn fought not to shut her eyes against the embarrassment. Those were not the words she was thinking in her head. Those words sounded more like *how've you been* and *how's the family*. Not, *let's psychoanalyze all of our previous actions.*

The question didn't seem to unnerve Justin. "Because I wanted to talk, say hello. See if we couldn't bury the past and be friends again." He held out his hands. "Friends. Just friends. Seems like twelve years is a long enough time to get over . . . things."

Yeah. If "things" were so simple. Still, even though the words sounded like they'd been rehearsed more than a few times, they struck something deep. "So you changed your mind? When you saw me?" *Was I not good enough?* No, she couldn't say it out loud. It sounded too much like her neediness that drove him away in the first place.

"No, it wasn't you. The timing was all wrong. Too many people crowded around." He tapped the hammer against the palm of his hand, watching it press his skin. "Felt like it needed more privacy."

"Privacy?"

"Look, let's just say," he exhaled loudly and looked over her shoulder toward Jennings Road and the thick woods on the other side, "I've spent a whole lot of time thinking and probably more time chewing on some pretty tough pride. I owe you an apology, okay?"

Taryn took a step back, then leaned forward. "What?" Surely she'd heard him wrong. He didn't owe her anything.

"The day we split up?" He slipped the hammer's handle into the back pocket of his blue jeans and walked past her to the ladder. "Know what? Let's just say I'm sorry. For everything." He jerked his thumb at the ladder. "I need to get a tarp out of the barn and get it up here before the rain starts."

Without any further explanation, he disappeared over the side of the house.

What did he mean by everything? If anybody should be throwing apologies around, it was her. She was the one who'd clung to him like a lost puppy. She was the one who'd begged him to give up everything to stay with her. Worse, she was the one who'd thought sex would get him to stay. One time was all it took.

No. If apologies were being handed out, they were all on her.

Maybe I've been silent too long. Jemma's words came back to her. Maybe they'd all been silent too long. If nothing else, he deserved to hear her say, "I'm sorry," even if she never told him how she'd saved him. Maybe then she could accept what he was offering, because suddenly, his friendship was everything she wanted.

Her foot found a firm toehold on the grass just as Justin's voice flew over the house. "Taryn! I found Jemma! Call 911!"

———

The wet floor of the waiting room nearly landed Taryn in a hospital bed herself. Her shoes skidded on the rain-slicked tile, and only Justin's quick reflexes and rapid arm around her waist stopped her from landing flat on her rear end in front of God and half of the small county hospital.

She didn't even have the wherewithal to be embarrassed. Jemma's ambulance stood empty outside, having beaten them to the hospital by several minutes. Several minutes they'd wasted in the driveway while Justin almost forcibly put her in his truck, insisting she was in no condition to drive. She refused to admit he was right, even though her shaking hands told her with every tremor she should have given in instead of wasting precious time arguing with him.

"You okay?" Justin slipped his arm from her waist and gripped her elbow lightly, guiding her to a chair in the corner.

What was he thinking making her sit down? Jemma was somewhere in this hospital, in pain. If Justin Callahan thought she was just going to take a seat and thumb through a magazine like some southern belle debutante, then—

"Taryn." He stopped in front of her, laid his hands on her shoulders, and leaned down just enough to put him smack in the middle of her field of vision. "Look at me. You're wound tighter than my great-granddaddy's pocket watch. Keep this up and you'll be in the bed right next to Jemma."

At least she'd know where Jemma was.

He eased her down to the chair, then took a step back. "Sit. Breathe. I'm going to go find out what's going on." Before she could come up with an argument, he was halfway to the receptionist's desk in the small ER waiting room, his rain-soaked boots leaving a damp trail on the floor.

Taryn closed her eyes and sat back in the chair. He was right. She had to calm down, or she'd be no good to anybody. But how could God throw so much at her in the space of ninety minutes and expect her to bear up? What next? Her grandfather rising like Lazarus?

Justin's footsteps drew closer, and he'd dropped into the seat beside her before she opened her eyes, afraid to ask. "How is she?"

"They just got her in. The receptionist couldn't tell me anything other than the doctor would be out soon." He sat forward, elbows on his knees, hands clasped. "Did you call Rachel?"

"She's coming as soon as she drops Ethan off at her parents' house." *Quick, Rachel, before I lean on Justin too much and drive him screaming into the rapidly darkening evening.*

"I'll hang out until she gets here."

No, he couldn't. It was too much like before, when he'd always had her back. When, in their last conversation, he'd told her the truth. She was too clingy. Too needy. She'd used him. Every word he'd said back then she'd deserved, and there was no way she'd sit here now, the first time she'd seen him in a dozen years, and let him think she was still the same girl. He might never know the depths of her strength or what she'd done to protect him, but he wouldn't ever again think she couldn't take care of herself. "I'm good. Rachel will be here in a minute."

"I'm not leaving you alone, so stop trying to fight me." He sat back and looked at her sideways, the smallest of grins tipping the corner of his mouth. "As I recall, you get your stubbornness right from your grandmother, don't you?"

"Yeah. This branch of the tree grew straight as an arrow." Taryn crossed her arms over her chest and tried to hold herself together. "What was she thinking climbing the rickety old stepladder in the barn? I thought she got rid of it two years ago when I gave her a new one for Christmas."

"You'd have to ask her. But every person in the county knows she's legendary for not asking for help."

Taryn shook her head. "She was hiding out there, you know."

"From what?"

"Me. You." This was a line of conversation they couldn't continue. Not now. The shock of seeing him again was still too strong, and this dash to the ER had her emotions on high. Talking about personal things with him was insanity.

"Know what? I'm fine." As long as someone came through the door soon to tell her Jemma was okay, it was the truth. If they came out and said anything different . . . A tremor shook her so she grasped her knees and held tight, afraid she'd fly apart if the vision fully formed.

"I've got nowhere to be. Dad rescheduled the Duncans when I called and told him what's going on with Jemma. He said to keep him posted." Justin stretched and crossed his legs at the ankles, boots shedding rapidly drying mud.

Every time the gray mud came into view, all she could see was Jemma's even grayer face as they loaded her onto the stretcher. Jemma lying on the ancient gray wood floor of the barn, arm at a crazy angle no arm should ever be, step ladder sideways on the floor as though it had jumped and skittered at a sudden sound. Or tucked tail and ran after dumping its precious cargo onto the old splintered wood.

When Taryn got home, she was going to break the stinking ladder into pieces and burn it in the old wood stove in the barn.

She pressed her fists against her eyes so tightly, white light swirled the darkness and imploded in a black hole sucking up all of the light in the universe. When she was a little girl, she used to press her palms against her closed eyes to see what would happen and to marvel at the play of light where there was no light. Now she just wanted the swirls and sparks to take away the sight of Jemma prone on the barn floor.

She shuddered again. *Please, God. Let Jemma be okay. If You take her, I've got nothing.*

"She was awake when they put her in the ambulance." Justin interrupted her prayer.

Taryn snapped her head toward him. "It would have been nice to know earlier. If I'd known, I'd have fought harder to ride with her."

"Exactly. And you didn't need to get in the way." He nudged his shoulder against hers. "She was talking slowly, but she was giving what-for to the EMT who was working on her."

"Oh, no." Jemma never missed a chance to tell someone else—in the most loving way, of course—how to do his job. "Was he not putting on the oxygen mask to her liking?" Knowing Jemma was responsive back at the house loosened one of the steel bands around Taryn's lungs, allowing a slight moment of relief.

"No." Justin turned his head toward her and smiled. "She has perennials in her flower beds by the pump house, and those boys had better be careful turning their monstrosity of an ambulance around, because if those begonias don't come back in the spring they'll be out there replanting every single one of them." His voice was deeper than Jemma's, but the tone was spot on.

Maybe the events of the last ninety minutes had made her hysterical, but Taryn barked a sharp laugh, drawing glances of reprimand from the handful of people waiting silently in the room and earning a sympathetic smile from the woman behind the information desk, who had probably seen everything at some point in her career.

Taryn smiled sheepishly and sat back in her chair. Jemma would be just the one to threaten a couple of burly paramedics with green thumb duty. She chuckled, and the heaving of her chest coaxed a tear out of her eye. She could lose Jemma. Could have already lost Jemma. Even if she survived, this was proof positive Jemma wasn't going to live forever after all.

Tears pressed into her throat, but she refused to cry in front of Justin. She studied the tip of her big toe where she'd scraped her shoe on a shingle on the roof. She'd like to go back and choose an alternate timeline, one where Justin told Jemma about the house and she railed for a few minutes, then went into the kitchen and started frying chicken and whipping mashed potatoes for dinner.

Taryn glanced at her watch. She should be washing up right now, getting ready to dig into something wonderful like mashed potatoes or squash, not waiting for a doctor to decide if a broken arm was the worst of Jemma's issues. "I'm sorry you got tangled up in this."

"No worries. It's not every day I get to rescue a damsel in distress."

She pretended not to understand his meaning. "Yeah, Jemma really needed you today."

He opened his mouth, closed it, then opened it again. "McKenna, your grandmother is the toughest bird I know. Jemma will be fine. She's probably back there telling the doctors they have no idea how to do their job the right way."

"True."

Before Justin could reply, the door on the other side of the room swung open. "Hope Brodigan's family?" A blue scrub-clad doctor glanced around the room. And he did not look hopeful.

5

Before Taryn could fully take in the doctor's expression, Rachel burst through the glass double doors on the near side of the room and skidded to a stop beside Taryn. Her hair hung in wet strings around her face, and her sweatshirt hung heavy and soaked from her shoulders. She wrapped an arm around Taryn's shoulders, breathing heavily and soaking Taryn's shirt with cold rain.

The gray-haired doctor bounced his eyes back and forth between them before they came back to rest on Taryn as though asking permission to speak in front of the crazy lady who'd just bolted in like a wild stallion during a hurricane.

She nodded, her absurd nervous giggle from earlier threatening to raise the curtain for an encore. "This is Rachel. My cousin. On my dad's side." As if the doctor even knew or cared.

"I had to drop my son off at my mom's," Rachel said lamely.

The doctor raised an eyebrow. Like the girl at the information desk, he'd probably seen it all at one point or another.

"How's Jemma?" Rachel finally reached the point where she couldn't wait any longer. Four seconds. A new record in patience for her.

Doctor Archer—Taryn scanned his name tag—fingered the business end of the stethoscope sticking out of his pocket. "She's just finished having some tests run and will go into CICU for observation as a precaution when she's finished, so you will only be able to go in two at a time for a few minutes at a time. We believe she experienced a syncopal episode. She essentially fainted. Her right radius was fractured in the fall, and she took a pretty good lick to the forehead, probably from the ladder or the floor itself."

"But she's going to be okay?" Now Taryn was the impatient one. She wanted to motion for him to speed up and tell her Jemma was going to be up and about and bossing everyone around and nosing into the whole town's business again in no time.

"She seems to be lucid, and I don't believe there is any lingering head injury, though we're waiting on the results of the MRI to tell us for sure. However, the blow to the head isn't our biggest concern." And then he stopped talking. It was as though he was hoping they wouldn't notice there was more to come and he could get off the hook from delivering the Really Bad News.

"What?" Rachel and Taryn were in stereo now, voices laced with impatience.

Dr. Archer pulled the stethoscope from his pocket and draped it around his neck. "She'll have to have minor surgery to reset the bone."

Taryn's shoulders relaxed. "Minor surgery?" Jemma had carpal tunnel surgery just the year before, the product of years of abusing her wrists at the sewing machine. Minor surgery? Taryn wanted to laugh with relief.

The doctor didn't appear to find it amusing. "For a woman with her condition, even minor surgery with anesthesia can be tricky."

Rachel tightened her grip on Taryn's shoulder, and their gazes met.

Taryn could feel her lip lift with confusion as she turned back to Dr. Archer. "What condition?"

His jaw tightened as his eyes flashed wider. "I'm sorry. I thought . . . You'll have to discuss it with her."

Pulling in a deep breath, Taryn squared off. "What's wrong with Jemma?"

A hand rested on her shoulder and pulled back slightly. Not Rachel. Justin. She'd completely forgotten he was still in the room. The fierce surge of anger ebbed, replaced by the irrational need to lean back against his solid chest and draw strength from him, a near stranger to today's Taryn. Something told her he'd be okay with it if she did such a thing.

Instead, she tilted her chin higher and faced the doctor. "I know. You can't tell me." She dragged her hands down her face and pressed her fingers against her mouth.

"When can Taryn see her?" Rachel finally spoke. She'd been quiet so long it made Taryn wonder whether her cousin had lost the ability to speak. The restless hyperactivity that blew in the door with Rachel had stilled into dead calm.

"Right now if you wish. But until we evaluate her head any further, I'd suggest against any sort of confrontation."

Taryn bit back a retort. There wasn't a confrontation planned. She just needed answers from her grandmother. Right now. Answers that would clearly have to wait.

Justin squeezed Taryn's shoulder and leaned forward, his breath tickling the hair away from her ear. "Want me to call Marnie? She'll get the prayer chain at the church started. I know she'll want to get here as soon as possible."

Taryn winced and nodded. There was going to be a high price to pay for not calling Marnie herself as soon as the ambulance doors closed behind Jemma. As her grand-mother's best friend and Taryn's confidante, Marnie stuck closer than family and would be none too happy they'd waited this long to call. "Please." She pulled her cell phone from her hip pocket and handed it to Justin. "Her number's in my contacts."

Justin stepped away, and the spot where his hand was on her shoulder cooled immediately.

She reached for his arm. "Justin?"

He turned, but the look in his brown eyes sucked away all of the words she was going to say. Taryn's jaw twitched back and forth, trying to form words before her brain landed on something guaranteed to make her look like a total loon. "Tell Marnie . . . Tell her to wait to come up here. I know she's a spitfire like Jemma and wants to march in here and take charge, but the time's not right. Not until probably tomorrow morning."

A grin as slow and sweet as warm molasses tipped the corners of his mouth. For an instant, there was a kindred spirit in the room, one who knew how her grandmother and her best friend were because he grew up with them, too. One who could imagine what it would be like to know the most invincible woman in your life had taken a hit that might be worse than it seemed. "I'll tell Marnie," he assured her. "I just can't guarantee she'll listen."

"She won't. Jemma wouldn't listen if it were Marnie up there in pain." Taryn chewed the inside of her lip. "Oh. And tell her there's no need to bring food."

Justin chuckled. "I'll tell her. But again—"

"You can't control her. I know." She gave him a soft smile and glanced over at Rachel, who eyed the two of them with interest.

Taryn shook her head slightly as Justin gave her shoulder one final squeeze, waved to Rachel, and stepped out the glass door into the parking lot, reminding Taryn just how cold the room was.

———

"If Jemma bumped her head and fractured her arm, why is she in cardiac intensive care?" Rachel's voice was low, almost drowned out by the sound of their footsteps in the hallway.

Taryn stopped walking. "What are you talking about?"

"He said she's in CICU. Cardiac. Heart." Rachel started walking again. "And he said she fainted. Since when does Jemma faint? Something's going on with her heart."

"This makes no sense. Other than the one issue she's had her whole life, there's nothing." It took a few of her own heartbeats before Taryn's legs received the brain's call to start moving again. Even then, they wobbled more than they should have. "Her last checkup was in May, and she came back and declared she was healthy as could be."

"May?"

"Yeah. Right before she went to Asheville to see her cousin." Taryn's feet dragged. "A sudden, unplanned trip to

Asheville. And she repeated it again in August. She was seeing someone at the hospital there."

This was why Jemma had taken to long walks through
the orchard in the early mornings. Why she'd suddenly
started telling Taryn where certain family valuables were
hidden, how to access her accounts . . . Why she'd led more
than one dinner table conversation about how she never
wanted to be hooked up to machines or left to waste away
in a nursing home.

The realization was just settling into a tremble in Taryn's
hands when they pushed through the metal doors of the
small CICU and found a nurse who led them to Jemma's
curtained cubicle.

Rachel turned to her before they reached the curtain.
"Let her rest. Don't bring this up tonight." Taryn opened her
mouth to protest, but Rachel held a finger up. "Don't." She
pulled back the edge of the curtain and ushered Taryn in.

Taryn didn't know what she'd expected, but it sure wasn't
Jemma sitting up in the bed, working a find-a-word puzzle
with her left hand, while her right lay wrapped in a sling
across her stomach. She slipped the pencil into the book
awkwardly and closed it when the girls appeared. "And
where have you two been?" The white bandage on her forehead crept toward her hairline in question. Far from looking
frail, Jemma simply looked like Jemma in strange surroundings, a penguin on the beach in Bermuda.

"W-waiting to come see you?" Taryn felt off-balance, like
she'd ridden a roller coaster too long and couldn't find her
footing.

"Well, here I am. Waiting for someone to get a lick of
sense and send me home. Foolishness, me sitting here in

this ICU excuse for a room when surely someone else needs it more than I do."

There it was. The perfect opening to ask why all this was necessary, but Rachel's elbow in the small of Taryn's back stopped her. If the doctor hadn't warned her and Rachel wasn't here to keep her in line, there'd be a whole lot of questions flying right now. Instead, Taryn curled her fingers tightly and redirected her words. "You can't come home 'til they set your arm. It would be more trouble than good."

Jemma wrinkled her nose and cast a glance at her arm. "Old lady bones. When I was your age, this never would have happened." She looked up again. "Rachel, I will be up and around in time to make the cake for your wedding. Don't you go worrying." She lifted her left hand. "My mixer only requires one arm, and Taryn can help with the finer points of the decorating. Soon as they cut me loose from here, I'll pull everything together. We've got a few weeks. All will be well." She reached out in the small space and patted Rachel's arm. "You just rest easy. I can't believe your wedding is less than a month away."

Taryn wanted to throw her hands toward the ceiling and scream. Jemma lay in a hospital bed under constant watch, and she wanted to talk about cakes and weddings?

Rachel patted Jemma's hand as if this was the most normal conversational setting in the world. "I'm not worried. And if you can't do it, it's okay too. Kerry's Bakery can bake a cake for me at the last minute if we have to. You worry about getting better."

Jemma "pshawed" her with a twitch of her hand, then turned her attention to Taryn. "I saw you up on the roof with Justin."

Oh, yeah. One more thing she and Jemma had to hash out. Probably one more thing she shouldn't bring up here and now too. The way things were going, she'd never get answers to any of her questions. Still, it wasn't the time to bring up the roof, not with Jemma's health on such a precarious ledge. "Jemma, why are you here?" The question popped out so fast Taryn's brain hardly registered it was going to speak.

Rachel gripped Taryn's wrist as Jemma's nostrils flared. "Because I fell off my stepladder, broke my arm, and banged my head."

No way was this the whole story. Jemma had a "tell" when she withheld information. Her face tensed so much in an attempt to look innocent that her wrinkles flattened out and she looked ten years younger.

"Not here in the hospital. Here in cardiac ICU. What's wrong with you? Why did you go to—"

"Not a thing is wrong with me other than a touch of osteoporosis making my bone weak. Let it lie."

"But Jemma—"

"Now, I need you to do me a favor." Jemma moved on, switching topics as fast as her mind could race. "I need you to bring me my makeup. And my curling iron." She tapped her thumb to her fingers on her left hand, ticking off the items as the list grew. "And hair spray. Please hair spray. Tomorrow when you come. I don't need to be in here looking like an old lady."

Rachel stifled a giggle beside Taryn and turned her eyes toward the ceiling.

"Know what I could use right now, though?" Jemma plucked at the stark white blanket. "One of those warmed blankets from the dryer. Those feel so good. Almost makes it worth being in here. I'm gonna have to remember when I go home and throw my blanket in the dryer every night."

Taryn was at attention before the sentence was even finished. "I'll go right now."

"Actually, Rachel, could you step over to the nurse and ask her for one?"

"Sure." Parting the tiny curtain, Rachel vanished.

Something was up. A couple of solid clicks passed from the IV next to Jemma before she spoke, her voice low. "I need you to work on Rachel's quilt for me. Get it finished." She lifted her hand and dropped it back to the bed at her side. "I'm good for nothing with my left hand. I mean, I could sew it, but even with my quilter's hoop it would be a mess. My left hand's just not steady with a needle."

She wouldn't deny her grandmother anything, but inside, Taryn groaned. Hand-sewing a quilt of such magnitude would take everything she had, every free minute after school. Not to mention hand-sewing was an activity she enjoyed about as much as a root canal. But she'd do it. Because Jemma had asked. Knowing her grandmother could see everything in her expression, Taryn arranged her words in her head before she spoke. "I've never sewn one by myself. I mean, I know my teacher was the greatest out there, but you've never set me loose all on my own before. And I know you've gone behind me in the past and resewn some of my stitches."

"Because I'm too much of a perfectionist. Believe me, little girl, you are a far better quilter than you think you are. You'd be surprised, and this has to be done. With her mama and her grandma gone and not able to do it, I promised myself she'd have a piece of her history on her wedding day.

And I want to keep my promise. Rachel deserves this after all she's been through."

Jemma was right, as usual. Taryn calculated in her head and knew she was cutting it close. "It's a lot of work."

"You can do it." Jemma said with a mysterious grin. "I'll be praying for you. And God just might send you some help from where you least expect it."

6

The packed dirt of the driveway held puddles of mud that squished and splashed under the tires. This brief break in the weather was scheduled to end with a sweeping cold front tomorrow night, and if this afternoon's downpour didn't dry before then, Hollings and the whole mountain would be in a world of slippery hurt. Up the hill, the lights on Jemma's roof twinkled above the trees, making the house look like a fairy gingerbread home. Jemma would love it if she could see it right now, sparkling away exactly like she'd pictured.

Taryn and Rachel had gone their separate ways in the parking lot of the tiny hospital. It wasn't until Rachel's taillights faded on the road up the mountain toward her parents' house the thought hit Taryn. Rachel would go home, call Mark, snuggle Ethan, talk to her parents . . . And Taryn would step into her tiny little house without even a dog to meet her at the door.

With her dash clock transmitting a blue 9:40, she'd decided to check on Jemma's house one more time to make sure the door was locked, stove off, dishes washed. Heaven knew, Jemma would definitely have a massive heart attack if dishes were left in the sink overnight.

Taryn smiled as her small SUV splashed through another puddle just before rounding the house. Guaranteed, Jemma would ask her about the dishes tomorrow, right after she asked if Taryn had brought her makeup.

The back lights shone brightly against the dark, illuminating the entire backyard all the way to the barn. They highlighted Justin's red pickup, sitting right by the back door.

Taryn's stomach dropped somewhere around her knees. What was he doing here? Asking the question kept her from acknowledging the tiny little flutter in her stomach. It was surprise, right? A jolt of shock at seeing a vehicle in the driveway. Not joy at seeing Justin. Not at all.

He rounded the house and leaned against the bed of his truck as she shifted into park. The instant Taryn opened the car door, Justin asked, "How's Jemma?"

"She's Jemma." The door slam echoed off the bare apple trees and blew back to her on the stiff breeze. "Wants me to bring her makeup tomorrow. You know, the usual. Forget she broke her arm and bumped her head and has some undisclosed medical condition she's refusing to talk about. It's all about not looking her age."

Justin grinned. "Makeup, huh? Yeah, I can see the importance."

"What are you doing here anyway? Shouldn't you be off somewhere sleeping or something?" She hip-checked the door shut and stepped up by the hood of her car, making sure to keep the two vehicles between them. Had she actually considered leaning against his broad chest in the waiting room? The heat creeping up her cheeks should have steamed in the damp chilled air.

"I don't need no stinking sleep. I had to come up here anyway, and I was kind of hoping you'd head up this way tonight before you went home." Justin reached in his pocket and held up an object.

Her cell phone. Great. Retrieving it would mean narrowing the buffer zone between them. They met at the front of her car, at the back bumper of his truck. "Thanks. I'd have been frantic here in a few minutes when I figured out it was missing."

"I thought about leaving it here, but where? And how would I tell you where it was? I have no idea where you're living, so . . ."

"In town. On School Street." She drew a line in the mud with her toe. He'd know exactly where her house was now.

"You're kidding."

Shaking her head, she smiled at the ground. Yep. He remembered.

"The little green house across the street from the post office? With the white fence?" A grin nearly split his face. "How did you manage that? You talked about the house your whole life. I never thought Wanda Jennings would give her place up."

"Wanda Jennings moved to Arizona to be closer to her grandchildren. And she didn't give it up easily. She rented it to me for a few years before she finally decided she'd never actually move back here. I had to promise her never to paint it a different color, so it will be green forever, whether I like it or not."

"Well, there ya go. Small price to pay for the house you always loved." He leaned an elbow against the tailgate of the truck. The stiff breeze fingered the longer hair on the top of his head, flipping it over itself and leaving it rumpled, reminiscent of all of those times he ran his fingers through it when he was nervous. Not a trace of nerves now, not in this man who held so much confidence Taryn envied him. "Never could figure out why you liked the place so much."

She shrugged and slipped her cell phone into her hip pocket. "I guess it just spoke something to me." What, she couldn't guess, but the tiny green house on the big town lot had first caught her attention before she could remember. Her childish eyes had been captured by the idea of a green house, sitting amidst the white-sided houses on the narrow Hollings street. Maybe it became a habit, staring at the color every time Jemma made a post office run, but it burrowed inside Taryn's heart and she knew she wanted to live there forever. Every time Justin and Taryn would bounce Fred through town, she'd detour by and force Justin to live her silly dreams of planters in the windows and an apple tree in the backyard. "Four years."

"What?"

"Four years ago, I bought it." The day she drove into Asheville and signed the papers making it—and a tidy little mortgage payment—hers, she'd had the irrational urge to call Justin, to scream out her triumph to the person she'd shared all of her longings with, even though it had been years since they'd last spoken. The tug was so big it scared her, and right now, it was back with an overwhelming force. Some small corner of her brain acknowledged she was playing with fire. "Know what? Thanks for bringing my phone. I need to go in and shut off some lights and make sure everything's secure. I'll see you later." The faster she got him off the property and out of her sight, the better.

"Actually, I still need to go up on the roof."

"At ten o'clock at night?"

Justin shoved his hands in his pockets and rocked back on his heels. "I never got the tarp done because Jemma . . . anyway, I was wanting to poke around a bit and make sure the rain from earlier didn't do any damage. I swung by Dad's and picked up a tarp and was just about to go up there and anchor it down. Won't take too long."

The dumbest thing Taryn could do while her brain felt like the scrambled eggs in fried rice was to tell him it was okay to stick around a little longer, but if she didn't and the roof leaked, she'd hate to have to explain her reasons to Jemma. And if she didn't let him go up there, he'd leave sure as the world, and she'd be right back where she started, alone, facing a dark house here and an even darker one at home. "I don't see a problem with you getting it done right quick." *Liar.*

"I'd just put the ladder up when I saw your headlights coming up the drive. Shouldn't take long." Justin flicked a two-fingered salute off his temple and disappeared around the house.

How could he be so nice? Act like she hadn't backed him into a corner and tried to manipulate him before he left? The way he treated her, sitting by her in the waiting room, showing up at the house to seal up Jemma's roof, it almost seemed like he'd managed to forget what she'd done. Why couldn't she let it go too? It would be so easy, would feel so good to just let herself sink into what they used to have, the solid feeling of Justin always being there for her.

If, in fact, he wanted her friendship back like he said he did. Why he would was beyond her. The only thing she'd ever done was use his time and his shoulder. Had she ever listened to him? Let him have his way when he wanted to do something?

Second chances. Did she deserve one?

Taryn tipped her head back and looked up at the sky, where dim stars peeked between clouds, harbingers of a temperature drop already painting the air. "Lord Jesus, I have no idea what I'm doing here."

He didn't clue her in.

With a sigh, she fished Jemma's house key out of her pocket and planted a foot on the cement back steps, just as Justin rounded the corner of the house, mouth set in a grim line.

"Taryn."

The key froze against the lock as her heart pounded twice. Had something else happened to Jemma? Why would the hospital call him? She stepped backward down the step away from the door. "What's wrong?"

"I'm sorry. I knew one bad rain could do some damage, but I didn't think it would—"

Taryn didn't wait for him to finish. The sewing room. Jemma had left Rachel's quilt on the machine table in the sewing room. She ripped open the back door, Justin at her heels, and raced upstairs.

Taryn ran her hands over the soaked fabric, bits of plaster and insulation clinging to her fingers. A tea-colored puddle soaked through the entire pile of fabric to the wood sewing machine table below, then dripped onto the rug over the hardwood floor. She closed her eyes and curled Jemma's hard work in her fist. "Ruined." The word leaked out on a moan. How was she supposed to go to the hospital tomorrow and tell Jemma that Rachel's quilt was destroyed, and there was nowhere near enough time for her to make a new one?

"Taryn?" Justin's voice was hesitant, like he was afraid she might punch him if he spoke too loudly. "I'm sorry."

Oh, it would feel so good to latch onto his apology and blame him for this mess, so good to take this whole evil, stinking day out on him, but one look at his miserable face and the idea died before the words could reach her tongue. He hadn't put the tarp on the roof because he was sitting at the hospital with her. Comforting her. She was the one who should be apologizing.

She sighed. "You can't control the weather."

"No, but I—"

Taryn threw her hand up between them. "Don't. Just stop now. It's not your fault." She dropped into the upholstered desk chair in front of the sewing machine, damp fabric cold against the back of her jeans. Well, now she couldn't stand up again without looking like a three-year-old after too many juice boxes. Why not add to the tally of yuck this day had already offered? She slid her hand along the damp fabric of the chair and held it up for Justin to see.

He winced. "Ouch."

The chair squeaked as Taryn leaned back, staring at the stain in the ceiling, plaster crumbling in damp splotches. "Well, I guess it could have been worse."

"I'd like to know how." Justin leaned back against the table, looked down at the water, made a face, and slid farther down to a dry spot before settling in again.

"I don't know. It's just what people say, isn't it?"

Dragging a hand down his face, Justin tilted his head back. "I'll fix the ceiling. No charge."

"Jemma would never let you. She'll probably go ahead and tell you to do all of the roof work once she knows what's going on. And don't you dare say one more time it's your fault, just because you caught it two hours before it fell in, young man."

"You sound just like her."

Taryn screwed up her lips and nodded. "I come by it honest."

"So what was up with the quilt?" Justin poked it with his index finger, lifting the edges of a stack of fabric as if to see whether the damage went all the way through.

"Rachel's getting married on New Year's Eve."

"I heard the two of them were finally tying the knot."

"On my dad's side of the family, it's been tradition for as long as anyone can remember for the mother of the bride to hand-sew a quilt for the wedding."

Her mother's voice still echoed, and Taryn could almost see her sitting in the middle of the bed on her purple and white quilt, sewn by Gramma McKenna, hastily, out of necessity. "Someday," her mother's smooth hands had guided Taryn's young fingers across tiny stitches, "I'll make one for you like Gramma made one for your dad and me and her mother made one for her. I'll teach you how to make one for your daughter. On and on, forever."

"Only Rachel's mother died in a car wreck. And you lost yours."

Justin's statement pulled her back into the room. "Yeah. And with Gramma McKenna gone when we were toddlers, there was nobody to pick up the mantle." She shrugged. "Jemma stepped in. It was going to be a surprise. Jemma

73

was worried she'd never get it finished in time, especially with Christmas coming on." She breathed out heavily. "The answer just became no."

"It has to be hand-sewn?" Justin pulled the least soggy piece from the bottom of the pile and inspected the stitches.

"At least the top part. Jemma said something about having the actual quilting done by machine."

"Hm." He held the strip of squares higher, close to his face, eyes squinted.

"Need glasses?"

"What?" The cloth dropped to the floor, and he bent to pick it up. "No. Just looking at the stitches. Jemma does a great job. Those are pretty tight, so close you almost can't tell they were done by hand. Can you clean this?"

"Doubtful." Taryn snagged her own strip and studied the soiled square. What had once been the brilliant white of new fallen snow now looked like the piles left in the parking lot of the gas station after all of the pretty snow melted. "It will always look like someone dumped coffee on it, even if you bleach it. Which you can't do anyway because it would destroy the blue." Satisfied she had headed off his next question, Taryn tossed the soggy mess onto the heap.

"Can you start over?" Justin added his own material to the pile. "Never mind. I already know the answer. Even if you didn't have to teach every day and visit the hospital, Jemma's probably been at this for weeks."

"Mmm-hmm. The tough part's not piecing together the rows, which is all we had left to do here. It's piecing the squares. On a sewing machine, I could get it done fairly quickly, but by hand . . . a queen-size quilt?"

"Too bad Jemma doesn't keep half-sewn quilts lying around."

"You are one funny guy, Callahan. Jemma Brodigan never leaves a project unfinished." The statement tickled a memory that drove Taryn to her feet.

"What?" Justin straightened, apparently ready to follow wherever she ran.

"Come on." Taryn paced out of the room, determined not to run out the door like one of her high schoolers on a sugar binge. She knew the exact answer to this problem. *Thank You, God.*

Justin clomped up the attic stairs behind her, never asking what was happening until Taryn had the quilt blocks spread out on the floor between them in a riot of green and white. He cupped his chin in his hand and shook his head. "You've got to be kidding me." One knee popped as he squatted beside her and picked up a piece of fabric, eyeing it in the dim attic light. "What's it doing up here?"

"I have no idea. Just found it helping Jemma unpack Christmas decorations."

"Well, it definitely qualifies when it comes to hand-sewn." Justin ran a practiced eye down the seams.

"Okay, wait. This is the second time you've talked like an expert." Taryn dropped onto her backside and wrapped her arms around her knees. "What gives, Callahan? The army teach you how to quilt and cross-stitch? Did you earn a medal for embroidery?"

"Very funny." He tossed the square into the pile and leaned back on his hands. "Remember when I broke my leg our junior year of high school and I couldn't do marching band?"

"Yeah. I was miserable without you." Wait. Those words sounded wrong. "I was miserable without you to cut up with at practice." A little better.

"I was miserable without you too." Justin cleared his throat. "Don't you remember what my grandmother set me to doing since I was of no use to Dad in the business or to the marching band on the field?"

Taryn snorted a laugh, the vision of Justin sitting at the kitchen table at his grandmother's house, awkward fingers holding a needle. "Hemming the shepherds' robes she sewed for your church Christmas pageant."

"By. Hand." Justin wiggled his fingers between them. "I never knew so much muscle ache in all my life. She only had the one sewing machine, so while she whipped out new ones, I hemmed the old ones." He flexed his fingers. "I'm here to tell you, I wished I'd broken both arms instead of one dumb leg."

"I remember now. Such moaning and groaning out of an almost grown man. It was pathetic."

"Hey." He lowered his gaze and aimed a finger across the unfinished quilt at her. "It hurt, okay? My manly fingers weren't made for a needle."

"Manly?" Taryn snorted. "Says the star mathlete and science fair champion of the Dalton High School Celtics?"

"Real men know pi to thirty-seven places."

"Okay."

His cheek cocked with a half smile. "Just so you know, you are still under threat of death if you ever decide to tell anyone. Ever. Because now I'm trained. By Uncle Sam."

Taryn tapped her eyebrow with a two-fingered salute.

"Anyway, it all worked out in the end. I will have you know being adept with needle and thread bought me many a meal during my time in the army. You'd be amazed at how many guys need pants hemmed before an inspection or a formal."

"I'd think you'd get laughed straight out of the barracks."

"I did. Once. And then I saved a few guys' butts from extra duty. Believe me, I was thanking my grandmother profusely every time I got a free pizza." He aimed a finger at Taryn. "Point is, I can sew a straight line pretty well, with stitches even enough to get a soldier past an inspection. I can help you sew these."

Taryn opened her mouth, ready to tell him no, but something stopped her. "I don't know."

"Why not?"

Taryn sniffed, shook her head, looked toward the window at the dark sky. "I seem to recall someone once telling me on his parents' front lawn how I was high maintenance and needy. This whole day is a fine illustration of both." There was no drama in the words, no emotion, just a stated fact. She'd long ago accepted he was right.

Wincing, Justin kicked the edge of a nearby plastic box. "Somebody was angry. And lashing out." He pinned her gaze. "Feeling manipulated."

"Rightly so." She couldn't meet his eye, dropping down to look at her feet instead, pulling at a loose thread on the hem of her damp jeans. "What I did was wrong. Way, way wrong." She'd wrestled with God about it more than Justin would ever know, but it was the first time she'd said it out loud.

"It was." His voice was too quiet.

The weight of conviction hit her like never before.

"It was devious and unfair." He said it matter-of-factly, emotion gone, probably long dead over years of thinking about what she'd done.

Taryn nodded.

He scooted around and planted himself right beside her, mimicking her posture, arms around his knees, hands dangling in the air. "But it was also wrong of me, losing my temper." He sniffed. "The older I get, the more people I get to know, the more I see it's better to hold your tongue and wait a little bit before you go off saying the first thing in your head. Mouth off and tell a drill sergeant just once what you're thinking about him, and you learn."

The air in the attic was suddenly heavy and still, but not in an oppressive way. It was like a warm blanket settled, comforting, peaceful, like Jemma's fresh-out-of-the-dryer hospital blanket. Did Justin feel it too?

He was inches from her radiating warmth that heated the chill in the legs of her damp jeans. "I knew better, and a tiny part of me even knew what you were doing, trying to convince me to stay, but sometimes, as a guy who'd already taken his share of cold showers . . ." His low chuckle held no humor. "There's a breaking point."

"I trashed our friendship."

"With my help."

"I'm sorry." *For so many things.*

"So am I."

So this was true confession time, in Jemma's attic. Not in any way she'd envisioned it so many times. Maybe now was the time to tell him everything, how she'd saved him, but she stopped. It sounded like bragging about her own sacrifice, like she wanted him to cheer her on and praise her decision. No. Now wasn't the time. The right time might never come.

But this time was here. He'd offered her his friendship. It was more than she deserved, and at the moment, she decided to accept it, to allow him back in just enough to fill the tiniest part of the hole left when they parted.

Justin leaned back on his hands again, behind her, so she couldn't see his face. "Tar, you'd be shocked if you had any idea what—"

Her hip vibrated, and it took a second for the buzz to reach her ears, to slice into Justin's statement. Without thinking about the rudeness until it was too late, only concerned something worse had happened to Jemma, she pulled the phone from her pocket and stared at the screen. "It's Marnie. I haven't updated her yet."

Justin bent a long leg and stood, stretching up to touch the rafters above him. "Take the call. I'm going to tarp the roof and head home." He looked down at her for a second, then nudged her shin with the toe of his boot. "You okay, McKenna?"

She nodded, and he vanished down the stairs, leaving the warmth of the attic behind.

7

Taryn tapped lightly on the wooden door. Earlier in the morning, before she could get back to the hospital, the doctors had moved Jemma to a regular room on the fourth floor. There was no indication yet what the doctor felt warranted the extra precautions, but apparently the situation no longer merited the constant monitoring of CICU.

The door swung inward to a large corner room with windows on two sides. Creamy beige walls met nearly identical floors. Taryn thought about asking how her grandmother had managed to get one of the most coveted rooms in the little Dalton hospital, but she already knew. This was Jemma. She could pretty much get anything she wanted with a well-pointed stare.

At the sound of Taryn's hesitant knock, Jemma looked up from the Bible on her lap. "Come on in. You brought my makeup, right? I'm sure I look a fright enough to scare some of these young nurses into their own personal hospital stays."

Taryn held up the small toiletries bag, then hefted a plastic grocery bag. "And I managed to sneak in your curling iron too. If you're a good girl, I'll let you use it."

"Hair spray?"

Taryn imitated one of the best *duh* looks her students liked to throw around. Who brought a curling iron and forgot the hair spray? Last time she checked, she was a girl. Girls remembered stuff.

Jemma finally broke her stern expression to smile. Ah. There was the Jemma only a few people got to see. "Well, bring them over here and tell me how things are at the house."

Now there was a loaded topic of conversation. Taryn glanced at the heart monitor beeping steadily by Jemma's bed and wondered what would happen if she told the whole rain-soaked story right now.

"You've only been gone overnight." Taryn passed the makeup bag to her grandmother and set the grocery bag on the floor by the bed. "Not a lot can fall apart in less than twenty-four hours." *Lord, forgive me for evading the question.*

"You cleaned up the dishes in the kitchen?"

Taryn's nod came with some hesitation. Yes, she'd cleaned up the kitchen. But only after Justin left and she sat down on the floor, wrapped her arms around her knees, and indulged in a good ugly cry over everything that had happened in the past two days.

Taryn looked away, out the window framing the mountains leading up to the high valley where Hollings nestled. For some reason, seeing Jemma lying in a hospital bed made her look like someone other than her Jemma. She looked ten years older, more frail. Taryn had never noticed the finer lines on her grandmother's face before, the fact her red hair had faded to pink and thinned in spots. All of these things became suddenly, starkly clear in the sterile beige surroundings. Taryn wanted to trade in the woman in the bed for her Jemma, the strong one who refused to ask for help when she needed a tool off the top shelf, who packed her pistol in her pocket to guard against any snake brave enough to challenge her as she set off for a daily walk through the orchard.

"Why on earth are you looking at me like I'm already dead?" Jemma demanded. "I cracked my arm, not my skull. Last time I checked, I was still breathing." The words were the typical tenacious Jemma, but her eyes weren't quite lit up like they usually were. Behind them lay an expression Taryn had only seen one other time in her life, when her grandmother hovered over her at the hospital in Pennsylvania. It was fear. Back then, Jemma was forced to face down one of her worst nightmares, her granddaughter following in her daughter's life-altering footsteps. Today, for someone who lived her life controlling everything around her, this confinement was likely tearing at her grandmother's sanity.

"You're going to be fine, Jemma."

"Eventually," she sighed.

"Has the doctor been in to see you yet today?"

"Not yet." The makeup bag rustled as Jemma busied herself pulling out foundation and other assorted gussying-up items. "He'll be around soon enough, I imagine." She smeared foundation on her face, then studied herself in the mirror of her compact. "My makeup's not too dark, is it?"

Taryn studied her face to placate her. They had this discussion about three times a week. "Nope. Blends perfectly."

Jemma eyed her granddaughter for a minute as if trying to judge truthfulness, took one more glance at the mirror, then snapped the compact shut. "But you'd tell me if it was, right? I don't ever want to be one of those old women who walks around looking like they glued an orange mask to their face."

"No danger of such a thing, love. You'd never let it happen. I think I'm more in danger than you."

Jemma looked up with a practiced eye. "Speaking of which . . ."

And here we go.

"Your blush looks a little bit pink. You might want to tone it down. Better yet, try another color entirely."

Taryn stood and leaned down to kiss Jemma's cheek. "You are so lucky I love you when you make comments like those."

"Like what? You don't want to walk around looking like a clown, do you? If I don't love you enough to tell you, who will?"

"Nobody loves me like you, Jemma." And nobody could make her angrier either. It said a lot about their relationship. They were probably closer than a grandmother and her granddaughter should be, but after all they'd been through together, it was bound to be a relationship just over the edge of the norm.

Still, it was time to change the subject before they wandered deeper into outward appearance. The inevitable next part of the discussion involved the fact that Taryn should never wear a baseball cap in public—not even to Walmart—and her shirts were too big and she should let her grandmother tuck the sides to show off her figure, which, come to think of it, might be a little heavy.

Taryn smiled in spite of herself. Jemma couldn't help it. She was born to boss, and she did it because she cared. It offended a lot of people, but it rarely offended Taryn. Rarely.

There had been a few knock-down, drag-outs between them. Usually after one of those "you look a little heavy" comments. If Jemma would stop inviting her over for spaghetti and caramel cake, "little heavy" might not be such an issue.

"So, we need to talk about why the doctor is concerned about you when they set the bone." Not the light conversation they needed at the moment, but Taryn couldn't help it. She had to know.

Jemma stopped rummaging in her bag and huffed a look at Taryn, a shadow crossing her eyes. "I'm past seventy. Anytime they put an old woman under anesthesia, they worry."

"There's more to it." Taryn sat forward in the chair and forced her grandmother to look her in the eye. "You're hooked up to a heart monitor. Pretty sure it's not standard operating procedure for a broken arm. Neither is cardiac ICU if they're watching a head injury."

"We can talk about it later. There's nothing new under this sun." Jemma plopped her hands on top of the bag and turned her full attention to Taryn. "Now, answer me a riddle that kept me up half the night."

Right. A riddle kept her up half the night. Not the mystery diagnosis or the pain she wasn't talking about, the same pain etching deeper wrinkles around her eyes and mouth. Taryn glanced at the IV and wondered how much medication was coursing through her grandmother's veins. Not enough, if she was this much like her old self. "What riddle?" Taryn dropped into the chair at the side of her bed and waited.

"Why was Justin the one to find me?"

Taryn's eyes drifted shut. The conversation on the roof seemed like it was another lifetime ago, overshadowed by the hospital and last night's ceiling disaster. It wasn't something they needed to get into now. But if Taryn didn't, Jemma would come after her when she found out. There would likely be no caramel cake for a long time as punishment. "He was coming in to talk to you about the house."

"What's wrong with the house? He got the lights up, right?"

"He did, and they were sparkling up a storm when I went by there last night. But Jemma . . ." Taryn leaned forward and stared at the rail of the bed. "The roof needs to be replaced. You have a hefty leak in one spot, and there are a couple more threatening." It was good enough for the moment. Hopefully, Taryn could get the replacement quilt done before Jemma found out the one she'd been working on so hard for Rachel was destroyed. "He was coming to tell you to get bids for people to do the work."

"Bids." She waved a dismissive hand. "Bids nothing. Have Justin do the work."

"I kind of figured you'd want him to. He's starting repair work today, but the roof will have to wait for warmer weather. I'll find out what he'll charge."

"Tell him to wait until tomorrow. There's never a good reason for work on Sunday."

Except a hole in the ceiling.

She charged on, thankfully not hearing Taryn's thoughts. "I don't care what he wants in pay. The income off the orchard will cover a gracious plenty. Now, I want you to know why I called Justin in the first place and not somebody else." Jemma laid her bag to the side before a sympathetic smile set in. "Sometimes we do things when we're younger, and we regret them later." The comment had an air of uncertainty a little out of character for Jemma. "Maybe it's time you two patched things up."

"I think we did." If the feeling of rightness in the attic last night was any indication.

"Good." Her smug look belonged only on a cat after it had filled its belly with pilfered tuna.

"Pride goeth before a fall, Jem."

Her grandmother opened her mouth to backtalk just as a sharp rap sounded on the door and an unfamiliar doctor poked his head in. "Mrs. Brodigan? I'm Dr. Sykes, the orthopedic surgeon."

The smug look slipped, and Jemma reached over to pat Taryn's hand. "I know you've got things to do today, and they don't involve sitting here with me, hon. Why don't you run on and work on Rachel's quilt for me, and you can come back and visit later this afternoon."

"But I just got here." And she wanted to know what the surgeon had to say.

"Run along." Jemma dismissed her granddaughter like a child. "You know how much Rachel needs her quilt. I love you. Talk to you later. Everything's fine."

⸻

Taryn's fingers burned from the long unfamiliar friction of fabric against skin, and they ached from guiding the needle through cloth to join green-and-white squares with solid white squares in an alternating pattern. In spite of the pain, the payoff felt huge. One entire row of the quilt was pieced together. A small surge of triumph numbed the ache in her fingers. Wow. And it only took her—she glanced at the clock on Jemma's white sewing room wall—four hours.

Her neck and upper back screamed from the unnatural position of hunching over in the chair. All she wanted was a good walk through the orchard, a hike up Jackson Mountain. Something, anything to move her whole body and stretch out tight muscles. Leaning back, she pressed her hands into her lower back and stretched, tight muscles telling how much she was going to hate them in the morning when it was time to get up and teach those high schoolers of hers.

There was still plenty of daylight left and a couple of hours before she went to see her grandmother again. It would feel good to pull on her boots and tromp through the orchard for a bit, let the fresh air kick out some of the fabric dust in her lungs, celebrate her triumph.

She dropped the sewn strip on the rest of the squares and deflated a bit. Some triumph. It took her four hours to sew one strip. The quilt needed about a gajillion more. At this rate, the thing would be done in time for Rachel's first anniversary.

A tap on the window nearly shot her out of her chair. She slid backward, losing traction on the plastic carpet protector, and gripped the edge of the sewing table, meeting eyes in the window. Fear completely ripped the scream trying to tear out of her throat, but then her eyes focused.

Justin. On a ladder. Laughing at her.

Taryn stalked around the table and shoved the window up, then leaned back against the table. "You're so lucky I learned the whole be nice thing in preschool, or else I'd shove the ladder away from the house and watch you land in the bushes behind you."

He looked over his shoulder as if gauging the distance, then shot her a boyish grin. "Wouldn't be near as funny as you scrambling just then."

The look Taryn fired at him should have knocked him backward without her even having to touch him.

"What were you doing up here anyway?" He propped an elbow on the windowsill. "I knocked, yelled, propped a ladder up against the side of the house . . ."

He did all that? Taryn kneaded a knot in her neck. "Guess sewing teeny tiny stitches in perfectly straight even rows requires more concentration than I thought it did."

"Why didn't you call me? I told you I'd help."

Because he only said it to be nice. Because the last thing a guy like him wanted to do was spend a Sunday afternoon when it wasn't brutally cold chilling out with a girl and shoving a needle through cloth. Taryn shrugged.

"Taryn, I meant what I said. Let me help." He pulled his arm from the windowsill and gripped the ladder with both hands. "I only came by to check on the tarp because I won't have the stuff I need to start repairs until tomorrow. I'm going to come around, and we'll work on the quilt for a little bit."

If she told him she was finished for the day, he'd think she was lying. Her aching fingers screamed a denial loud enough for him to hear, but it was nothing compared to the lecture he'd likely give if she didn't let him help. "Okay."

"Don't sound so excited," his voice drifted back up to her, and the ladder rocked against the house as he disappeared.

It was only a minute before Justin appeared in the doorway. He slapped his hands together like they were about to play ball. "Needle? Thread? Let's get this quilt pieced."

Taryn wanted to be mad at him for being as bossy as Jemma, but she couldn't. The sight of him, broad-shouldered, square-jawed, and military tall, calling for a quilt to be pieced was more than her frayed emotions could handle. She laughed like he'd morphed into Abbott and Costello combined with the Three Stooges. She laughed like only laughter could save her life.

And maybe it was true.

The thought sobered her up pretty quickly. The mirth was gone as quickly as it came. "Sorry, Sergeant Seamstress." A smirk sneaked out.

He eyed her, one eyebrow raised, arms crossed over his chest, making his biceps strain against the fabric of his long-sleeved t-shirt.

Yeah, again, this was not the Justin she grew up with. Taryn looked away before she could enjoy the looking too much. She gave up the right long ago. They were friends now. Friends. *Friends.*

"Are you finished laughing at me?" The question was laced with sarcasm.

"I think so." Yep. She was definitely finished. The warm little fuzzy in her stomach was nothing to laugh at.

"Can we sew now?"

She choked on a snort.

"Whatever." Justin dropped his arms to his sides and stalked across the room in what Taryn hoped was mock anger. "Give me a needle. I'll sew you under the table."

"Sounds uncomfortable." Jemma's glider rocker slipped back and forth as Taryn sank sweetly into it, then reached for a stack of squares on the table beside her. If her fingers had tear ducts, they'd weep.

"You know what I mean." Before Taryn could even re-thread her needle, Justin was settled on the floor, threaded and stitching.

Pain or not, the challenge was on.

They worked in silence for nearly twenty minutes before Justin finally spoke. "How's Jemma today?"

"Cantankerous." Taryn pulled her thread through and gauged how many more stitches were left before she had to reload.

"Jemma? Cantankerous? No."

"Sarcasm is not becoming, Mr. Callahan."

He whipped her a grin and made two quick stitches. "I was kind of surprised to see your car here. I figured you'd be at the hospital with her."

"You and me both."

"So what happened?" Justin's thread popped as he snapped it and reached for the spool on the sewing table.

"She booted me out when the orthopedic surgeon showed up."

There was a long silence as Justin rethreaded the needle and found his last stitch. He probably whipped through five or six stitches before he stopped and caught Taryn looking at him. "What are you not saying, McKenna?"

"You've been doing that a lot."

"Doing what a lot?"

"Calling me McKenna." When he was six years old, Justin had decided he wanted nothing more in life than to be a soldier. For more than a year, he refused to call people by their first name because his Uncle Roger called all of his Army buddies by their last name. Until his mom jerked a knot into his rear end, he even called her Callahan. The habit died off after a while, but it was a joke the two of them carried into high school.

"Army training? Old habit?" He laid his half-finished strip aside and leaned back on his hands, stretching his neck and straightening his legs in front of him. "I've outsewn you twice over. What's going on?"

"The surgeon had something to say, and she didn't want me to hear. She ousted me because of it."

"Did you ask her about it?"

"Yeah. And she changed the subject." Laying the pieces aside, Taryn gave up on sewing and flexed her fingers. They'd done plenty for the day, more than she'd have gotten done if she'd given up when Justin arrived. "It's her heart."

"You're sure?"

"Yeah. She was born with a congenital condition, hypertrophic cardiomyopathy. Basically, the lower part of her heart doesn't pump right. I think it's gotten worse. She took a couple of mystery trips to Asheville earlier this year, right after her doctor's appointment, and then she talked more than ever about not ever wanting to be hooked up to machines. She actually had a living will drawn up, with the provision the will overrides any decisions I'd make as her agent."

"So you can't reverse what she wants." Justin folded his length of cloth and laid it on the sewing table. "She's scared."

"What makes you say she's scared?"

"It's why she's kicking you out. She's afraid of dying or burdening you. I know because my grandmother was the same way. She'd rather face this on her own than drag you into it too."

"She should know better." The light outside shifted, a telltale sign the clouds bringing in snow were building. Taryn pushed out of the chair and slipped behind the sewing table

91

to press her nose against the glass and stare out at the mountains rising beyond the orchard, tops obscured by clouds. Just a small part of the picture was all she could see. "My whole life, Jemma's been right there, first for Mom and me, and then for me. Even in the worst time of my life, she was right by my side, not letting me hold anything back." She whipped back toward Justin, buried in anger at her grandmother for not letting her in. "I'm going to go to the hospital and force her to do the same." Jemma was going to have to pay attention to her and let her know what was going on. She was going to the hospital, coming snow or no coming snow, to have this out with her. Her grandmother was going to tell her, or Taryn was going to pin her doctor in his office until he revealed it all.

"She'll never tell you, especially if you go blasting in there with your guns blazing."

"Must you be the voice of reason?"

"Someone has to be." There was a rustle and a creak. He'd settled into Taryn's vacated rocking chair. "Give her time. She may be just finding out herself what's going on. She'll sort it all out and get to you when she's ready."

"You seem to know a whole lot about how my grandmother operates."

"Yeah, well, I spent almost as much time over here as I did at home growing up. It only makes sense."

Taryn looked over her shoulder at him, his ankle resting on his knee, chair gliding back and forth. He looked like he belonged, which was a problem. The conversation was getting way too comfortable. Last night, close proximity nearly drove Taryn to tell him everything. Neither of them was ready, especially with her emotions all out of whack.

Letting this renewed friendship move too quickly would be the height of stupidity.

"Thanks for your help this afternoon." Taryn turned and leaned against the windowsill, letting her gaze rest to the left of his eyes. "You need to get up on the roof now and do whatever it is you came over here to do, and I need to go see Jemma and get ready for school tomorrow."

The chair glided back and forth a few more times before Justin said anything. "Shutting the door on me, huh?"

"No." The walls came up. Did he learn the crazy mind-reading thing from Jemma, or was she just easy to decipher? "I have a lot to do."

"Okay. If that's how you want to play it." He shoved up out of the chair and headed for the door, stopping halfway and keeping his back to her. "I'll be working up on the roof tomorrow, but when you get done with school, I can help you with the quilt again."

"Don't worry about it. I think I've got it covered. I'll probably take it home and work there." The farther she was from him, the better off they'd both be.

His shoulders stiffened. "Okay. See you later." Without looking back, he stepped through the door, the stairs creaking as he walked away.

8

"So what do you think I should do?" Chelsea Shope, one of Taryn's eleventh-grade world history students, twirled a brown curl around her index finger and waited for some kind of inspired wisdom.

The words sounded like they had to swim through pea soup to reach Taryn's brain. The weekend had caught up with her this morning when her alarm went off. She should have taken the day off like she'd threatened until Jemma talked her out of it. *What are you going to do? Sit around here and stare at the old woman in the hospital bed all day?*

One more week and Christmas break would take away one stressor, but only one. The rest loomed like a mushroom cloud in the distance.

If Chelsea could read Taryn's mind, she'd know her teacher was as uncertain about life as any high school student was. Taryn could remember when she was Chelsea's age, thinking her teachers were all so much older, they had some mystical grip on their lives, and one word—*adult*— made life so much easier. Even in high school, Taryn had this vague notion all the grown-ups did was teach at school, go home and do more paperwork, then go to bed. It never occurred to her they had friends and dates, went to the movies, and ate popcorn like everyone else did.

Of course, if Taryn's kids thought all she did was shuffle papers at home and live a life filled with history, they'd be right.

"Ms. McKenna?" Chelsea's voice sliced the cake of a growing pity party.

Taryn looked down at her student, a thin waif of a girl with gorgeous thick brown hair and huge brown eyes, her jeans perfectly faded and her shirt from a store whose clothes Taryn would never be able to wear . . . not since she was out of her twenties.

But this was not about her. Taryn sat down on the desk next to the one Chelsea had chosen. Chelsea was the cutest little thing with a sharp mind and quick wit, and here she sat thinking she wasn't good enough because one arrogant jock threw her over for a cheerleader when she wouldn't sleep with him.

Usually, when the girls came to her after school wanting to talk, it was about friends or family or popularity. Those were pretty easy. All Taryn had to do was adjust her thinking and remember what it was like for her in high school, then she'd give the advice she wished someone had given her. This time? Taryn was so not the one to be giving guidance to Chelsea on this one. Not when she'd been the one to pressure Justin into sex the summer after they graduated. Just the memory made her want to crawl under the desk and hide.

But Chelsea had come to her, and the last thing the girl needed was for Taryn to shut her down. "Know what?"

Chelsea turned soft, hurt brown eyes to Taryn. "What?"

It was time to dig deep into her reserves. "I hear you. The whole situation stinks. And I'll tell you a secret . . ." Taryn glanced at the door and wondered if her job was worth what she was about to say. If Chelsea ever repeated the words about to come out of her mouth . . .

She fired up a quick prayer for wisdom. Yeah, the risk was worth it if, for one moment, Chelsea felt like somebody else got it. Taryn knew enough about the girl's home life to know her parents sure didn't get it.

Surrogate mother. Just one of her many unwritten job descriptions.

Chelsea leaned forward the smallest inch, waiting to hear what "secret" her history teacher was going to lay on her.

Taryn bit the inside of her lip. "I'm human, okay? And when I look at Dylan . . ." She couldn't believe she was about to say this to a student who, in a fit of "knowing" could run out and repeat it to all of her friends. But this wasn't the first time Chelsea had come to her with a problem, and she'd never run to her friends before with what Taryn said. "Dylan cares about one thing. Dylan. He's got the fastest car and the hottest clothes and the greatest hair . . . Everything about him is about having the best. He's used to getting everything he wants, which seems great, but people who get everything they want are rarely ever going to be happy." Taryn slid off the desk and rested on her heels in front of Chelsea, so she could look up into her face. "They are never going to see beauty or worth in anything, Chels. They are just going to keep wanting the next thing. For a while, you got to be the next thing for Dylan, until he couldn't have everything he wanted from you. You stuck to your convictions and told him no. You may be the first person in his life to ever tell him no."

Tears gathered in Chelsea's eyes. "It was so good to be loved though, ya know?"

Taryn's heart squeezed tight for the girl in front of her who had no idea of her own self-worth, who was measuring it in terms of what a boy could give her. She hurt for the younger Justin and for putting him in the position where he had to say no . . . A no she'd refused to hear, hoping it would make him stay. She'd been just like Dylan, using sex to gain control. Except where Dylan had used it as grounds for rejection, Taryn had used it in a desperate bid to make Justin stay with her. Her eyes drifted shut. *Dear Lord, I'm so messed up. What in the world can a hypocrite say to this girl?*

Chelsea didn't seem to notice Taryn's internal crisis. "The most popular guy in school wanted me. Me, who can't even get her parents to notice whether she's home or not. Do you know how it feels? To have someone tell you they love you when they don't have to?"

Did she ever. Taryn just nodded.

"And then to find out it was all about sex? And some other girl is better than me because she'll give him everything he wants?"

It took every ounce of Taryn's strength not to wince. She wrestled her own guilt to the side and forced all of her attention onto Chelsea. *God, help me.*

In a flash, it came. This was not about sex. It was about the self-worth of a girl whose parents never told her how valuable she truly was. "Remember last year, Dylan got his Mustang when he turned sixteen?"

Chelsea nodded and swiped at her eyes with her fingertips. "Everybody loved the Mustang."

"And what's he drive now?"

97

She snorted. "He talked his parents into an awful, ugly jacked-up truck. I hated riding in it when he'd pick me up."

"Exactly. Look. Just because Dylan thought something else was better didn't make it better, did it?"

Chelsea's eyes gleamed in a new way, a small flame of amusement flickering behind the tears. "Are you calling me a Mustang, Ms. McKenna?"

"I'm sure not calling you a jacked-up truck."

Brown waves bounced on Chelsea's shoulders as she nodded. "I think I see what you're saying."

"Just because Dylan moved on, it doesn't make you worthless. If anything, it makes you the smartest, bravest chick I know for standing your ground." Taryn flicked Chelsea's knee with her finger and stood to look down at her. "Can I say the grown-up cliché here?"

Laughing, Chelsea flipped her hair over her shoulder. "Go ahead."

"Don't let other people determine your value, Chelsea. You're amazing on your own. And don't think you have to have some guy to tell you. There are more than three hundred boys running around in this school, and they all want different things."

"I thought they all wanted the same thing," Chelsea muttered, cheeks pinking.

Taryn choked on her next words. "Um, out of *life*. They all want different things out of life." She aimed a finger at her student. "Watch yourself."

Chelsea rewarded her with a smile.

"The point is, you'd have to mold yourself into three hundred different Chelseas if you wanted to date all of them. Be Chelsea. Live your life for God, just like you've been doing, even when it's as hard as this. When and if it's time, love's going to show up. And when it does, it will probably be when you aren't looking for it and you least expect it. No matter what, it will be worth it when the time is God's and it's right." Taryn tapped Chelsea on the forehead with her index finger. "Love isn't something you earn. It's not something you have to be good enough for. Real love is freely given, not taken away because you don't do what someone wants."

A tap on the doorframe lifted Chelsea's head and drew Taryn's attention.

Marnie stood in the doorway, gray hair windswept. "Am I interrupting anything?"

Taryn glanced at Chelsea.

Standing, Chelsea shouldered her backpack. "Nope." She took two steps, then pivoted and leaned over to give Taryn a quick hug. "Thanks, Ms. McKenna. You helped." As she strode across the room, her head just a little higher than when she came in, she gave a quick, "Hello" to Marnie and disappeared around the corner.

Taryn slid onto the edge of the desk and turned her gaze to the ceiling. *Thanks, God.* Those words to Chelsea sure weren't hers. She looked back at Marnie. "So, what brings you by the school today?"

"One of the grandbabies had a basketball game today and left one shoe in the backseat of my car. I don't have to tell you how high school boy brains can be." Marnie stepped into the room and leaned her shoulder against the white-board, leveling a gray-eyed gaze on Taryn. "So, were you talking to Chelsea or to yourself just now?"

"What do you mean?" Taryn eased off the desk and stooped to retrieve a wadded piece of paper from the floor. One of the perils of confiding in her grandmother's best friend? Having two senior citizens who thought they could read her mind. "It had nothing to do with me. Dylan Bradley dumped Chelsea in favor of Anna Snyder."

Marnie winced and held up her hand for Taryn to toss the paper to her. She caught it neatly and dropped it into the trash can by the door. "Ouch. Anna was the head cheerleader this year, right?"

"And how would you know the inner goings-on at this high school?"

"High school boys gossip just as much over dinner and pie as high school girls do." Marnie grinned. "So, Anna the cheerleader was suddenly better than Chelsea the softball star?"

"You got it." Never would Taryn violate Chelsea's confidence by telling the whole story, even to Marnie.

"I'm going to tell you what. Dylan Bradley has wreaked havoc on some of the girls in my daughter's Sunday school class. Some days I'd like to take him and shove his head into a locker."

Taryn chuckled. The scary part was, Marnie might take it upon herself to do such a thing. "Okay. A locker bashing from you wouldn't earn you anything but a front-row seat to a lawsuit."

"Yeah, but when I look at some of those girls . . ." Marnie plopped down on the edge of the seat of the desk Taryn had been sitting on earlier. "How many broken hearts has he sent running to you this year?"

"More than a few."

"These girls gravitate to you, Tar. God's sent you here for a reason, you know."

Taryn shrugged and kept straightening the rows of desks, snagging a pencil someone left in their chair. God wanted her to minister to girls? It was more likely their wounded spirits probably attracted each other. "Whatever you say, Marn."

"Hm. How's Jemma?"

"Ready to come home."

"I went by the hospital last night. I had to check my back-seat twice before I pulled out of the parking lot to make sure she hadn't hitched a ride with me somehow."

"Sounds about right," Taryn said. "She's going stir-crazy."

Marnie slid farther back in the desk like she was settling in for a good long chat. "So with everything going on, we haven't had the chance to talk. Word has it Justin Callahan was your waiting room support system the other day."

Not this. Not now. The gossip train did speed faster between small towns. Taryn plopped stacks of notebook paper homework onto her desk and pulled the frayed edges from one formerly spiral-bound sheet, then flipped her file case open and slipped the papers in by class period. If she kept moving, she wouldn't have to look Marnie in the eye. "He was at the house hanging Christmas lights when Jemma fell, and he drove me to the hospital. There's nothing more to it." She kept her voice light. The last thing she needed was Marnie asking questions about things she couldn't even puzzle out herself.

Marnie leaned back and crossed her ankles. For the most fleeting instant, the grandmother of six looked like she could be one of Taryn's high school girls. "So let's go back to my original question." Marnie slid out of the desk and crossed to where Taryn stood. She yanked open the bottom desk drawer and went straight for the Peppermint Patty stash.

Taryn shook her head. The woman's sweet tooth was worse than Jemma's. It had to have roots all the way down to her toes.

Handing Taryn a piece of candy, Marnie popped half of another piece into her mouth and swallowed. "Was the conversation earlier about Chelsea or about you?"

"I told you. It was about—"

Marnie held her hand up between them. "I meant the line about love finding you when you least expect it. You certainly weren't expecting Justin back."

Taryn stopped pulling silver foil off her candy. "You know better than to go there, Marnie."

"And I've held you enough when you cried after the two of you parted ways." Leaning back against the filing cabinet, Marnie crossed her arms and tapped a work-worn finger against her bicep. "You're hiding from him."

"No, I'm not." Because if she was, she certainly wouldn't be letting him sew on a confounded quilt with her, wouldn't be letting him make her laugh, wouldn't be looking forward to the next time he showed up without warning. Taryn unwrapped the rest of her candy, then popped it into her mouth. Cold peppermint sifted all the way up into her sinuses, but it did nothing to cool her head. What was she doing playing with fire by letting Justin get close? In order to have him back in her life, she'd have to tell him the truth about Sarah. And if she told him the truth about Sarah, she'd likely lose him anyway.

No matter how Taryn played it in her head, there was no way for her and Justin to have a happy ending.

9

So, what are you thinking?" Rachel's voice had the tone only her voice could have. Cute and cheerleader without being the least bit cloying, even at twenty-nine. The girl had never known a bad day.

Taryn shut the cabinet door and sighed, feeling like a lifetime of bad days. This had to stop. Maybe it was all of the cloudy weather and the unseasonable amount of snow flurries. Seasonal affective disorder, maybe. It couldn't possibly be Jemma in the hospital and Justin peeking into her life, bringing up all of the things she'd managed to, if not forget, at least shove aside. "I'm thinking tuna and," she peeked into her fridge, "yogurt. Likely mixed together."

"You just dropped two notches below disgusting."

"I know. But I forgot to go to the grocery store this weekend, what with everything going on, so I'm pretty much down to the basics." The days had fallen into a routine. Work. Visit Jemma. Come home, grade papers, and sew Rachel's quilt. Food was pretty low on the priority list.

"It's Wednesday. Rita's serving pork chops at the grill in town. She doesn't close 'til eight. Get your coat, walk two blocks, and have some real food. I'll bet you haven't eaten a decent meal since Saturday."

True, but Taryn wouldn't give her cousin the satisfaction of saying so.

"Speaking of which," the phone rustled as though Rachel shifted, "how is Jemma today? I meant to get over there this afternoon, but I wound up with an emergency session."

"She's ruling the roost. Got the nurses hopping to her bidding and thinking it's a privilege to do so."

Rachel laughed. "I think Jemma is going to be just fine."

It was infectious. "Yeah. When I left, she had talked them into bringing her an extra dessert and tea in her little bed-side pitcher instead of water."

"Seriously?"

"Yep."

"Hey, listen." Rachel paused as a microwave beeped across the line. "Ethan and I are chilling out tonight. Mark's on duty at the fire station in Dalton, and Mom and Dad are at church. Ethan refused to nap at preschool today, and I wasn't about to foist him on whoever had the nursery tonight. We're feasting on leftover squash, corn, and pot roast. Come over, and we'll watch a movie after he goes to bed." There was a crash and a squeal. "Which will be soon."

It sounded so tempting. Time with Rachel, not sitting in her own quiet house with too much time in her head, but there was a ton of quilt work to do. "Can't. I skipped church tonight to sew, and I can't give up the time."

"Sew? Did I hear you right? Since when did you take up sewing?"

Taryn winced. She needed more sleep if she was going to keep the filter on her mouth tight. How should she answer?

"Jemma had a quilt special ordered. She needed help getting it done in time." True enough.

"Gotcha. Need a hand?"

Definitely not. If Jemma found out Rachel had laid one second of work into her own quilt . . . "I'm good." She wasn't, but she couldn't say so. At the rate things were going, it would take four hands to get this thing done in time.

Someone rapped at her front door. "Who in the world?"

"What?" Rachel spoke louder over another Ethan squeal in the background.

"Stay with me a second. I've got someone knocking."

"Probably Marnie wanting to know how Jemma is."

"Nope. She was at the hospital when I left." Taryn reached for the corner of the curtain in the den and peeked out.

Justin's truck sat behind her small SUV in the driveway.

Something wiggled in her stomach. Hunger. It had to be hunger. "It's Justin."

"Treat him nice, Tar." Rachel hung up before Taryn could ask what she meant.

Justin knocked again. "I can see you peeking out the curtain. You can't pretend you're not home."

Taryn jerked the door open so fast, Justin took a step back. She leaned against the door frame and crossed her arms, aiming for a nonchalance she was pretty sure she couldn't hit. "Stalker much?"

"Am I coming across like one?" For the first time since Friday night, he looked less than confident. "Seriously?"

"Depends on why you're here."

"I brought pizza." He reached over to the rocking chair by the door and produced a thin box. "Ham and pineapple."

He remembered. "Keep talking."

"And," Justin passed the pizza to her and dug into his front pocket, producing a small, silver object. "A thimble."

"I have a thimble." If she deliberately misunderstood him, maybe he'd let her keep the pizza and leave. It was best for them both, even though the thought of him retreating and backing his red truck out of her driveway left her heart feeling even emptier than her stomach.

"It's mine, McKenna. I promised to help, remember?"

Taryn was powerless. Old habits died hard, and the old habit of hanging out with Justin, of being friends with him, took over the new truth. This friendship was probably dangerous. She stepped aside. "You're just in time. I was about to see how peach yogurt would work in tuna salad."

"You're kidding, right?" Justin stomped his work boots off on the mat and stepped through the door, instantly shrinking the small living room just by stepping foot on the beige carpet. He leaned down and pulled his boots off, setting them outside on the porch. "You know, I've never seen the inside of this house before, even though you talked about it forever when we were kids."

"Well, this is it." Taryn slid the pizza onto the end table and walked to the fireplace to flip on the gas logs. She needed distance. It felt too normal, him showing up unannounced with food. It had happened a hundred times before. He had a way of making it feel like time and circumstances had never changed, of making her want to sink into the fairy tale and pretend everything could go back to the way it used to be.

"How's Jemma?" Draping his work jacket over the back of the chair next to the door, Justin stepped cautiously toward the middle of the room. "I like the little bit of orange in the paint. Just enough to make it warm and not white, but not enough to make it a creamsicle."

"You are way too much of a girl."

"No." He grinned. "It's my job. Dad's had me work on quite a few remodels in the past. Fixing to start one now down in Dalton, one of the old mill houses by the river. I've been up to my eyeballs in paint colors the past few days. Between Jemma's roof and this remodel, I haven't been able to get over here sooner. But I did get the patches on the roof finished today. She'll still want a reroofing in the spring, but it's tight 'til then."

"You're finished?" This explained his mysterious absence. "And there's another job since the roof is done? Awesome." Her smile couldn't be helped. "As for Jemma, she's the same. They set the break in her arm yesterday, but they're keeping her for a few more days. She was ornery about it today because *White Christmas* is on TV Saturday night, and it's our tradition to pop popcorn, shut off the lights, and watch it together. The cable at the hospital doesn't get the channel."

"It's a bummer she'll miss it."

"Yeah."

"She told you why they're taking all of these precautions yet?"

"Nope, but I talked to the doctor long enough to figure out it's definitely something with her heart condition. They were worried the anesthesia wouldn't play nice with it."

"She'll come around and tell you when she's ready." Justin took a step back and scooped the pizza box off the small end table. "Kitchen?"

"This way." Taryn headed for the short hallway leading to the back of the house, floor creaking with each step. "I'll take you back. I think I can only offer you water to drink, though. And we can eat out here. Maybe we can catch the weather and see if they're forecasting for Christmas yet." Something about eating at her tiny kitchen table with him felt more intimate than it should.

"I doubt it. You've still got two weeks." His stockinged feet thudded lightly on the carpet behind her as she headed up the hallway. "Still holding out hope for a white one, huh?"

"Always." Did he have to remember everything about her? And did he have to be so nice? She popped open a cabinet door and pulled down two glasses. All it did was remind her how, unless she told the truth, he could never be hers. But if she told him the truth, he wouldn't want to be hers, anyway.

———

"And he screamed like a little girl." Justin leaned back in the recliner and laughed at the memory only he could see.

Taryn bit back a laugh of her own. "Dude. You put a snake in the man's sleeping bag. That's the opposite of funny. It's like, death, it's so not funny."

"The snake was dead when I found it." Justin's laughter took over again.

"Okay, but your battle buddy or whatever you called him didn't know it was dead." The last word tore on a giggle. It was so infectious, the way Justin laughed, with his head back and his brown eyes crinkled. She'd forgotten how nobody could keep a straight face around a Justin who got tickled by one of his own jokes. Just like when he was a kid. *How come it's raining today? How come? Because all of the clouds had to go potty!*

Boys.

"Aw, once he got over the fright, he laughed too. What wasn't so funny was the team leader catching us and making us do extra duty the next day. But it was worth it. And two days later," he sat up and reached for the quilt row he'd set to the side when he started his story, "there was a dead scorpion in my bunk."

"Nice."

"Yeah." His voice trailed off as he went back to pushing needle through fabric, sans the thimble he'd decided two hours ago was just not worth the effort, or the humiliation when Taryn had threatened to take his picture.

Taryn stitched three or four stitches and stopped, watching Justin work. He looked almost comical, his work-hardened muscles hunched over a quilt square, but here he sat, two hours in at almost ten at night, helping her.

No. Helping Jemma. He was here because he was helping Jemma. This had nothing to do with Taryn.

"What?" He kept urging needle through fabric, never looking up.

"Huh?"

"I can feel you looking at me. What's up?" He snapped a thread, then reached for the spool on the floor beside his chair without looking at her.

"You miss it, don't you?"

He threaded the needle and sewed a handful of stitches, his eyebrows drawn together, before he finally stopped and looked up. "Yeah. I do. Parts of it."

"Like?"

"Brotherhood. Having a cause to fight for. Excitement." He shrugged. "Jumping out of airplanes for fun and paycheck."

"So why leave? You could have stayed in. There's nothing here in North Carolina for you, right?" Taryn bit the tip of her tongue. It sounded like she was fishing with her question, and maybe some part of her was. She slapped it partway into hiding in the back corner of her brain.

Justin eyed her, his face unreadable. "You don't know?"

Why was it suddenly hard to swallow? She reached for the abandoned and cold cup of coffee beside her and swigged bitter chill. "Know what?"

"My dad." Gone were the laughter and the teasing.

Taryn's heart jolted. "What's wrong with your dad?" If something had happened to Justin's father . . . She was sure she couldn't take any more bad news, not with Jemma being all mysterious from her hospital bed.

"He found out earlier this year he has Parkinson's."

"Justin, no." Taryn's hands fell to her lap, the needle pricking her palm. She jerked it away and inspected for blood. Not Justin's dad. In her memory, he was so tall, so strong, like Justin. Always in motion, always helping, hauling around construction material like three men lived inside him. And always, always smiling. "You're just like your dad." It seemed odd to think of it now, but seeing Justin more mature made the connection to present and past clearer than ever.

"I hope so." It was said with more conviction than she'd ever heard out of him. It should be. His dad was everything hers wasn't. For the first time, she saw what else she'd lost when she'd lost Justin. His family. "What happened?"

"He started getting dizzy spells. Falling. Didn't take much to figure it out." Justin dragged his fingers heavily along his jaw. "He's early on, but he's getting tremors enough so he can't work like he used to. And if I hadn't come back," he shrugged, "well, he'd have had to shut down Callahan Construction."

"Oh no."

"I always planned to come back home. Someday. Believe it or not, there are things for me here other than Dad and the business. It's just I didn't think it would be so soon. I sort of thought I had more time. But at the same time, I was always worried time would run out on me." He shook his head and sat back in the chair, focused on the flickering gas flames in the fireplace. "But yeah, I miss the army. Sometimes. It's just not something I talk about a lot. I've only been out a couple of months. It'll probably get easier."

"I guess." Taryn needed a break. Needed to walk out of the room, to process the thought of Justin's strong dad being felled by such an ugly disease. Needed for him not to see the tears trying to crowd up on her. This wasn't her pain, it was his, and he didn't need to be comforting her. She snatched her mug and stood, scattering thread and quilt pieces to the floor and sliding the couch back a good two inches with the force. "Coffee?"

Justin glanced into his mug. "I'm good. But I'll take some water." He moved to stand.

Taryn waved him down. "You keep sewing. You're faster than me. I'll be back in a minute." She bolted for the kitchen like someone was chasing her. Popping a cup into her single-serve coffee maker, she hit the button, leaning against the counter as the machine whirred and heated. Here was Justin, more mature, more confident, more everything good . . . and she hadn't changed at all. She'd been so all about herself since he stepped foot back into her life. She had no idea he was hurting just as much as she was. She was the same selfish, self-centered, needy teenager as when he last laid eyes on her.

So why was he hanging around?

111

To help Jemma, she reminded herself. And nothing more. Taryn filled a glass with water, grabbed her coffee mug, and headed back for the den, resolved to be better.

Justin hardly glanced up when she set his glass on the table next to him. "Thanks."

"Yep." Settling back on the couch, Taryn drew her knees up to her chest, blowing on her coffee. "Was it hard, the army? Deployment?"

Justin let the quilt drop into his lap and reached for his water. "Do you know I've missed almost every single Christmas at home for the past eleven years?" He took a sip, watching her over the rim of his glass.

Taryn hesitated, then nodded. She knew. Well. Every year, something in her looked for him, half hoped he'd pull up in the driveway just to say hi and see how she was doing. It never happened. Until this year, and now she didn't know what to do with it.

"It was always something. Training. Deployment. Stationed too far away. For a few years, it was by choice." He shrugged and set the glass aside. "Feels weird, being here. Weird, but right." He looked at her again. "I'm doing the right thing."

"You are." His dad needed him. Justin wasn't the type of guy to turn his back.

His smile edged with a sadness Taryn couldn't quite puzzle out. "You know the guy I was talking about with the snake and the scorpion?"

"Yeah."

"We were stationed together again this last deployment. I was in Alpha Company and he was in Bravo. We were on BPs about seven miles apart in Kandahar."

"BP?"

"Battle position. Like an outpost. We used to get rocket-propelled grenade fire just about every day." Justin set the recliner rocking slightly. "His mess tent took a direct hit. In July. He was gone before the smoke even cleared. Him and three other guys waiting for chow with him."

Taryn inhaled sharply. "I'm sorry."

"Right after, Dad found out he had Parkinson's, and it all got me thinking." He took another sip of water, set the glass down, and picked it up again. "Well, just leave it at—it got me thinking. Probably too much." He drained the glass, then got up and headed for the kitchen, not looking at her as he passed. "Need anything?"

"No." She watched him retreat, probably for the first time in his life. All she could do was sit there, wait, and wonder how to respond, how to be there for him right now while he needed her.

He came back a different person. "You haven't decorated your house yet?"

"When?" If Justin wanted to change the subject, it was his prerogative. "Decorating usually doesn't get done until Christmas break anyway. There's one more week before I'm free."

"Still, no tree? No manger scene? Not like you, McKenna."

No, it wasn't, but with just her to enjoy it, the decorations seemed to get put up later every year. Some years, it was more trouble than it was worth, even though she liked coming home to a holiday-inspired house. "I'll get to it."

"Maybe I'll bug you until you do it." As Justin dropped back into the recliner, he laced his fingers and straightened his arms in front of him. "Okay, ready for another set? I'll race you. See who can get five squares sewn in fastest." He reached for his stack as the house phone rang.

113

Taryn snagged the portable from the back of the couch, grateful for a few seconds in which to process his mood swing. "Hello?"

"Taryn? This is Audrey Reynolds at Dalton Community Hospital."

Taryn's whole body grew colder.

"We need you to come in."

10

Why is it so cold in here? Taryn wrapped her arms around her middle and doubled over in the fake leather chair, head between her knees. The muted brown of the CICU waiting room's carpeted floor did absolutely nothing to settle her stomach. Instead, it made everything worse. The pizza she'd scarfed with Justin wasn't sitting well, even though it should have digested hours ago. It threatened to reappear at any moment. "Why'd they call me here just to make me wait?" Justin had ushered her through the hospital doors half an hour ago, and they'd been directed to the CICU waiting room, where dim lighting in the windowless room did nothing to soothe her mind.

"I don't know. I'm guessing they're getting her settled. The doctor said it was a minor heart attack."

A heart attack. One of Jemma's worst fears. Next to Alzhei-mer's, it was the thing she worried about most. "She's probably up there somewhere scared right now."

"Jemma's tough. She's going to be okay." Justin laid a hand lightly on her back and, when she didn't pull away, the touch settled there, making small circles between her shoulder blades.

The man must have a whole lot more respect for her grandmother than she'd ever given him credit for. It wasn't long until midnight, yet here he sat, waiting to hear how Jemma was. "You can go. I know you have a ton of work to do tomorrow, and you can't back out on it. The business needs the money. I'll be okay." The words muffled against her knees. She was used to doing things alone. It was her life. "I already called and arranged for a sub tomorrow. I can stay all night if I need to."

"Go home? And leave you with all of this excitement? Not on your life. Can't let you have all of the fun, can I?" It was a flash of young Justin, who everyone believed never had a serious thought in his head, but who allowed Taryn in enough to see how deeply his mind ran, how seriously he perceived life. "Why do you do that anyway?"

"Do what?"

"Pull away. Try to stand up all by yourself. Shove back everybody who wants to help you." The circles on her back grew heavier. "You try to push me away. You told Rachel not to come. At some point, you're going to have to accept people care about you and want to be there for you."

Because you told me once I was too needy. Yeah, it was a conversational path best left untraveled tonight. Right now, the only person who had never let her down, had loved her unconditionally, was suffering, and she couldn't get to her.

Yet, here sat Justin. If Taryn closed her eyes, she could easily believe the past few years hadn't happened and this was high school, where they normally sat side by side supporting each other. But this wasn't high school, and a whole lot more had happened than Justin Callahan could ever guess.

The fact didn't stop nostalgia from leaping up as a defense mechanism. "Do you remember during our sophomore year when Grampa took Jemma to Ireland?"

The circles on her back hesitated, then his fingertips tightened. "I do." Justin's voice deepened, then he cleared his throat. "You fractured your wrist during phys ed."

Silent tears pushed forward into Taryn's eyes, burning the back of her nose. "Dad told the school to handle it. He wasn't leaving work to deal with my clumsiness."

"As I recall, Wayne Demmings all but tackled you diving for a foul ball. Trying to be the hero as usual." He sniffed. "It was the only time I ever almost got into a fight. At least in high school."

"I never knew."

Beside her, he shifted until the toe of his work boot came into her view. The edges were caked with dried mud, probably from Jemma's driveway after working on her roof all day. The same driveway where he'd helped Brandt Foster load Jemma's stretcher into the ambulance just a handful of days ago. "Yeah. I thought he was a little too aggressive with you. I also thought he should apologize."

"He did. Later." She thumbed away a tear threatening to break away and bathe her cheek. "Now I know why. You scared him."

"I doubt the trombone-playing mathlete I used to be was scary. And what would you expect me to do? He hurt my best friend. Then he laughed about it." From the motion of his hand, she could tell he shrugged. "Not much else I could do, was there?"

"How long did you sit downstairs in the ER waiting room with me, waiting for me to get x-rays and all?"

Another shrug, then his fingers moved back and forth slowly, like he was thinking. "I don't remember."

"You do too. It was something like four hours. It was the middle of a huge flu outbreak, and the place was packed. They were too busy taking back all of the puking people to worry about the girl who wasn't creating a huge mess all over the room."

"It was pretty nasty. Thanks. I'd managed to forget the details."

Another tear edged to her eyelash. All of this time, she'd been so angry at Justin for telling her the truth, so dead set on protecting him from her mistake, that she hadn't realized how much she missed him until he was back in her life. She'd swallowed and buried all of the good they'd had. What had they lost the night when she crossed the line, let fear of being apart drive them to do something they'd never done before?

And why was it he suddenly felt the need to be in her life again, helping her sew a quilt, of all things? Sitting here with her in one of her lowest moments. Simply being right where she needed him to be when she needed him to be there. *God, this is not funny.*

The teenager in her wanted to lean over like she had so many times before and let Justin Callahan put an arm around her. She wanted to trust the strength in his chest and the comfort of his words. But the adult Taryn knew better. He'd been right back then. She could get needy, get too wrapped up in other people doing for her. If he'd taught her anything, it was how to stand on her own two feet, and for that she'd always be grateful.

In fact, it would be better if she got her legs under her right now. Taryn stiffened her spine, and Justin's hand stopped its motion. With a deep breath she sat back, forcing him to withdraw his hand.

From across the small waiting room, a pastel painting of dim pink tulips in a faded cream vase stared back at her. Somebody needed to update the decor around here. It grew more faded every second, like she felt. Wilted and tired.

"You okay, McKenna?"

She wanted to say yes, but when she opened her mouth, the tears took it as an open invitation. "No." The one word undid every bit of the bravado she'd built up. She could stand on her own two feet, but not if it meant standing without her grandmother.

Justin engulfed her in a hug, pressing her face against his shoulder. He smelled of sawdust and outdoors. After she had exhausted her tears all over his cotton shirt, she knew, for the rest of her life, the combination of smells would be more comforting than any bowl of soup, vase of flowers, or warm hug could ever be.

She drew away, cheeks flaming hot over making a complete spectacle of her fear and grief. While her family was loving and affectionate in private, they were not so into public displays of anything. Taryn had just violated the top eight rules of conduct. Good thing nobody was in the small waiting room to see.

Well, nobody but Justin, who probably wished he could go home and take a shower before the salt of her tears dried into a crust on his shoulder. "I'm sorry."

"For what?" He drew back but kept his arm around her. "Being human?"

"Being needy."

Justin's arm stiffened, but he didn't pull away. Instead, he leaned closer. "I told you. My mouth got ahead of me, and the things I said to you were wrong. I was too young to even realize we were feeling the same things, just acting on them in different ways." He drew in a deep breath, pain etching lines around his mouth and along his forehead. "God knows how much I wish I'd kept my mouth shut. Have you been carrying my stupid words around all this time?"

"I don't want to talk about it." Taryn pulled away, letting his arm slip from her shoulders. "Not now." She wasn't going to let him feel bad for saying what was true. It had taken all she had to keep the baby from burdening him, and she wouldn't undo it all by becoming a burden herself. "I'm fine. It's the doctors you should worry about." She forced a smile. "Like you said the last time we were here, Jemma's probably got them jumping through hoops and telling them how to do their job."

The comment drew a weak, if reluctant, smile. "You're probably right, especially if you're quoting me. Then you're definitely right."

"I just hope Daniel Markham isn't on duty. She's still not convinced he made it all the way through PA school."

"Daniel Markham will be lucky to get through the door of Jemma's room after the way he threw you over at homecoming to go to the dance with Shelly Banks."

Another reminder she could have done without today. "It was pretty nasty. Thanks. I'd managed to forget the details." She echoed his earlier words.

"Hey, it worked in my favor. Wasn't long after when you decided you might just love me as something more than your best friend." Justin's chuckle was familiar, yet strange all at the same time, and it died quickly. "Know what? I'm sorry all of this is happening." His voice dropped deeper, and he sounded somehow older, maybe even wiser.

Taryn refused to look him in the eye. If she did, he might see she was starting once again to view him as more than a friend. She rubbed her arms through her sweater, wishing she could warm up, knowing the chill likely came from inside her. "I can't lose Jemma, Justin." She stood and turned around to stare at the wall behind her, never looking down. She hadn't met his eye yet. She couldn't. "I never had my dad, lost my mom, lost you, lost . . ." Her eyes drifted shut, and she knew her cheeks had to turn pink. Enough. She had to stop talking. If she didn't, she'd tell him everything.

Maybe she should. But before she could open her mouth to speak, another voice took precedence. It was like a rerun of Saturday, only this time, a female doctor peered into the room. "Are you Taryn McKenna?"

The idea that answers were here, answers she might not want, shot adrenaline through her heart. "Yes. Jemma? I mean, Hope?"

The young doctor smiled. "You can come with me. We've tucked her back into CICU as a precaution, but she's going to be fine." She looked over Taryn's shoulder at Justin. "Are you family also?"

"He might as well be." Taryn glanced back at Justin, and he smiled slightly.

"No. I'll let Taryn go on her own this time. But, McKenna," he looked hard at her. "I'll be right here when you get back. Promise."

Taryn had to be trapped in *Groundhog Day*. She'd done all of this before. Followed the doctor up the silent hallway, stepped through the CICU doors into the room of curtained partitions, peeked at a Jemma hooked up to more than one machine . . . Her worst nightmare. Jemma's too.

This time, there was no crossword puzzle book. Jemma lay back in the bed, looking tired and small under the blankets, her good hand resting on the cast over her stomach, face creviced with lines and valleys Taryn couldn't ever remember seeing before. She wanted to back out of the curtain and tell the doctor there was a mistake—someone had put an old, old lady in Jemma's bed.

"Are you going to stare at me all day or come in?" The voice was strong and impatient.

Nope. Taryn couldn't help smiling just a bit. This was definitely Jemma.

"It was a tiny little heart attack, not a full-out burst artery." The frail hands moved, gaining strength, and the head of the bed rose slightly. Jemma eyed her with those striking blue eyes of hers. "Took you long enough to get back here."

"You know they wouldn't let me in 'til you were settled. And they'll only give me a couple of minutes now. They have rules, you know. I can't just charge back here whenever I want."

"Rules." Jemma swished her hand toward the curtain. "Suggestions are what they are."

Taryn pulled the small plastic chair in the narrow corner up closer to the bed and sat down. "Tell me what's going on. You fall and break your arm, they stick you in cardiac ICU. You have surgery, everything is grand, and then you have a heart attack."

"Not a heart attack. A mild heart attack. They made you wait while they did the EKG. They'll let me out of here and back into my room tomorrow morning as long as I'm stable. And I will be stable, so stop your worrying."

"Well," Taryn sat back and crossed her arms, "excuse me for worrying when they call and tell me you're heart attacking yourself. Clearly, you're just fine."

"And so are you, if this much of your sarcasm is showing." Jemma grinned at her, the old lady who'd overtaken her bed when Taryn walked in disappearing rapidly, though she still looked tired.

"I get it from you, dear." Taryn sat forward, resting her elbows on her knees. "Now tell me the whole truth, including why they stuck you in CICU from day one, and why they didn't let you go home right after setting your bone. You've been here way too long for someone who just broke a bone, even if you are seventy plus and counting."

"Fine." Jemma gave up too quickly, her fingers picking at the edges of the white blanket. "You know I've always had an issue with my heart, the one I was born with."

"The HCM." Taryn nodded, scared to hear what was coming, relieved to finally find out what was going on.

"Well, on top of it, I've started having blood clots. They're not related and nothing major. Small ones, but enough to put me on some medication. It's why I fell out in the barn. I got dizzy on the ladder."

"I threw the ladder out."

Jemma sniffed and shook her head with a tight smile. "Took out your anger on an inanimate object, did you? I trust the ladder. We've had it for years."

"Exactly why it needed to be replaced. I couldn't find the one I bought you for Christmas a while back, so I got you a new one. Aluminum. It's lighter. Won't rust. Won't wobble either. It's waiting for you in the barn when you need it again."

"Wobbly or stable, nothing would have kept me from falling this time. It was all the light-headedness from the anti-clotting meds. They kept me here longer to make sure I hadn't bruised enough to make another one." She shrugged delicately under the thin hospital gown. "Turned out to be a good call." She tipped her head toward the IV bag hanging on a stand next to the bed. "A little stronger clot buster in there. It'll keep me in here a few more days, but hopefully, I'll be home by Christmas."

"And resting."

"Now, Taryn," Jemma tipped her chin and raised one eyebrow, a look Taryn recognized and dreaded, "you know that won't happen, no matter how much I promise the doctor otherwise." She held up a hand to stop Taryn from speaking. "No more arguing. I'll remind the nurse you're in here, and she'll have you out on your rear before you can blink twice."

Taryn kept her mouth closed.

"Now, how is Rachel's quilt coming along?"

How was the quilt coming along? It was wreaking havoc on her life. Giving her a near panic attack by getting destroyed. Giving her a guilty conscience for not telling Jemma exactly what was going on. Giving her a divided mind by forcing her to spend time with Justin, time that had clearly had an effect on her heart.

She shrugged, hoping to look nonchalant and convincing, or Jemma would be all over it, reading her mind and figuring out everything Taryn was trying to hide. "It's coming. Rachel will have a quilt for her wedding, even though your arm is out of commission." *It just won't be the quilt you think it is.*

"I know you understand why this is important. With Rachel losing her mama, I want her to have something to make her feel like her mama and her grandmother are there at the wedding." The grin Jemma flashed almost made Taryn fear for her facial muscles. "Can you imagine the look on her face when she sees it? It will be worth every second of work."

Taryn's fingers ached to argue, but they couldn't. Jemma was right, as usual. Seeing Rachel's face would make every stitch worth it. "You're going to be responsible for ruining her makeup."

"Pshaw. She won't open it until after the wedding's all over and they're opening gifts. She won't worry a whit about her makeup by then." Jemma sighed. "I just wish I'd broken the left arm instead of my right one. Then you could bring me the quilt, and I could work on it up here. You could dig out my quilting hoop and set me right to work. It'd keep you from doing it all by yourself."

"It's okay. Justin and I are making progress on it." Oops. In her rush to console, Taryn had let too much slip.

"Justin and you? Together? Well, now." Jemma crossed her good arm over her casted one, the look on her face defying Taryn's efforts to read it. "What an interesting turn of events. I had an idea he'd be around fixing the roof, but I had no idea . . ." She tapped her index finger on her hot pink cast. "Very interesting." She didn't look like it was interesting, more like it was a little bit concerning.

"Don't go getting any ideas in your head, hon. You know nothing can come of this." If it was the truth, then what was the . . . thing . . . she kept feeling? Like every time Justin was around, the world seemed a little bit more right? *Lord, don't let Jemma be able to do the face-reading thing she does on this one.* "He was helping me sew the quilt, nothing more. But then I had to come here and make sure you weren't about to check out of the world on me, so we had to take a break so he could drive me over here."

"He sews?"

"Better than I do if you want the truth. His grandmother was Sissy Callahan. Of course he sews, and you well know it."

"It's because you're in a bigger hurry to finish, and you aren't trying to find pleasure in the doing."

True. But she didn't have to admit to it. "I promise. Rachel's quilt will be one you can be proud of."

Jemma shifted in her seat, the fire back in her eyes, though the lines around the edges said she was tired. "What time is it?"

"A little bit past midnight." Taryn stood. "I should go. You need to rest. I already got a sub for tomorrow, so I'll be around in the morning to check on you."

"You didn't have to. What are you going to do? Sit and play checkers with the invalid?" Once again, she held up her hand to ward off Taryn's protests. "So it's near midnight, and Justin was at your house to bring you here? Sewing a quilt? Have you two finally buried the hatchet?"

Taryn gripped the bed rail so hard her knuckles ached. "I don't know, Jem." Justin had, but Taryn could still see the handle sticking up out of the ground, waiting for her to trip over it.

Jemma laid her free hand on Taryn's. Her skin was cool and dry against the heat of Taryn's muddled life. "Tell him the truth."

Looking down at their hands on the rail, Taryn shook her head.

"Until you do, nothing good can come of the two of you together. You may have done the right thing for both of you, but sooner or later, it's going to come out. Better he hear it from you than from someone else."

"You and I are the only two in Hollings who know. Who's going to tell him? Why do anything different now?"

"Things change. Circumstances change." Jemma looked away at the curtain. "It will always be between you, and you'll never be able to trust each other." She gripped Taryn's fingers tighter. "Tell him."

"You were the one who convinced me not to let him know in the first place, telling me it was better if he didn't know." Taryn pulled her hand from her grandmother's grasp. "Why the change of heart?"

"Age begets wisdom." Jemma sighed.

The nurse poked her head around the curtain. "It's getting late, ladies. Ms. McKenna, would you like to come back in the morning? She should be in a regular room by ten or so, and you can stay as long as you want."

Taryn nodded, glad to drop the conversation she wasn't ready to have with anyone yet. The conversation she'd likely never be ready to have with anyone ever. She pressed a kiss to Jemma's cool forehead and slipped through the curtain with a promise to come back tomorrow.

Her hiking boots thudded softly on the tile floor of the hallway as she headed back to where Justin waited. Life had been good. Though it wasn't perfect, the routine had been comforting. Why did Justin have to come back and complicate everything?

11

"Sooner or later, somebody's going to have to bring me a steak." Jemma stuck her fork in the chicken breast Taryn had baked and brought to the hospital for her. The utensil stood in the meat like a flag pole of surrender. All they needed to do was tie Jemma's napkin around it to complete the look.

"Something wrong with the chicken?" Taryn cut another bite and held it up to look at it. She had to agree with Jemma. Plain chicken breast wasn't appetizing. Some honey barbecue sauce would go a long way toward helping the matter. Still, she'd smelled the food cart as she passed, and this had to be better.

"Wanna know what's wrong with the chicken you're studying? It's not a T-bone."

Taryn laughed. "It's not Jell-O either, so eat up or I'll go hunt down the nurse and have her bring back whatever it was she tried to bring in here earlier."

"Smelled like dog food. Sick people need good food, not bland cardboard that Fido would turn up his nose at."

"Well, aren't you cranky tonight?" Taryn couldn't say she blamed her. They were marking a week of Jemma being in the hospital, and Christmas was creeping up ever faster. It had only been three days since the minor heart attack set her back, and with each passing day, Jemma's mood got worse. "You need to get a little bit of Christmas cheer so they'll let you come home."

"Hard to get Christmas cheer when the walls are beige, the sheets are white, and my skin is looking grayer by the day. Look at this." She held out her good arm. "I'm losing my tan."

"What tan? You've been wearing long sleeves since September. There wasn't any tan left when you came in here."

Jemma slouched against her pillows and huffed her indignity at the world. "It's the point of the matter, Taryn Margaret."

"Honey, I've seen two-year-olds who've missed their naps over at the church preschool less petulant than you are right now. When they get like this, the teachers make them stand in the corner."

The edge of Jemma's mouth twitched. "I'd sure like to see you try to put me in a corner. You'd find out just how much strength this old woman's got left in her."

Taryn pointed a finger at her grandmother. "Ah. There's the Jemma we all know and love."

"You found the Jemma we all know and love? I didn't know she was lost." The voice from the doorway turned both of their heads. "To mutilate a time-honored eighties quote, I thought nobody put Jemma in a corner." Justin stepped into the room with a wink at Taryn, his arms loaded down with a plastic grocery sack and a canvas duffel bag.

What was he doing here?

"What have we here?" Jemma flung a quick glance at Taryn, then held an arm out to Justin for a greeting. He set the bags on the floor beside her bed and obliged her with a quick kiss on the cheek before turning to Taryn.

She jerked away as he ruffled her hair before he reached for the bags. "Well, Justin. What brings you by today?" She hadn't seen him since he dropped her off at her house in the wee hours of Thursday morning, although he'd called a couple of times over the course of the past two days to check on Jemma's progress and see how the quilt was going. With the remodel he'd taken on in Dalton, his time was eaten up well into the evening. Taryn had sewn alone the past few nights after coming home from the hospital, feeling out of sorts, already used to having him around.

She was in so much trouble.

Justin hefted the duffel bag and set it in her lap. "Christmas cheer."

"Do tell." Jemma leaned to the side to try to see around him.

"It's Saturday night, right?" He flashed a grin at Taryn and jerked his chin toward the bag. "Open it."

It seemed the grown-up Justin was full of more surprises than the young Justin ever was. Every day, he shocked Taryn one more time. She unzipped the bag cautiously, wary of spring-loaded snakes or mounds of confetti and gasped softly when she realized what was inside. "Jemma, you won't believe . . ." She looked up at Justin's eager face. "You didn't."

"Let the old invalid woman see." Jemma planted a hand on Justin's bicep and eased him to the side, her eyes widening. "A DVD player?" She leaned as far as she could over the edge of the bed, her grin widening every second. "And the movie." Her voice dropped low, but her smile widened. "How did you know?"

Justin settled gently on the foot of Jemma's bed and braced his hands beside him. "Taryn let slip the other night you were afraid you'd miss y'all's tradition of watching *White Christmas* together. I double-checked and, sure enough, the hospital doesn't get the classic movie channel. They told me I could bring a DVD player and hook it up to your TV if I wanted. Nobody should have to miss Bing Crosby and Rosemary Clooney at the holidays, so here I am."

"Now all we need is popcorn." Jemma looked like a kid on Christmas morning, her smile genuine and wide for the first time since the ambulance loaded her up and brought her here.

Something told Taryn that Justin had taken care of snacks. After all, he'd thought of everything else. "There's popcorn in the grocery bag, isn't there?"

"If you want to call it that. I asked about popcorn, but the nurse said you could only have air popped and plain. So you got air popped and plain." He leaned down and picked up the bag, then settled it on Jemma's lap. "It tastes like packing peanuts to me, but it's the thought that counts, right?"

Jemma sighed happily and peeked into the bag, then pulled out a plastic container filled with popcorn. "Justin Callahan, I have sorely missed having you around. Your mama raised you right."

He mimicked Jemma's trademark hand wave. "Pshaw. You're just saying nice things because I brought you Bing Crosby and popcorn."

Popping a kernel into her mouth, Jemma nodded. "You could be right there, but it has been too long, hasn't it?"

Taryn wanted to kick her right in the shin. What was Jemma thinking? Could she be more matchmaking than she was right now? Well, fine. She'd turn the tables on her grandmother one-two-three. "Jem, stop flirting. He's less than half your age."

Justin choked on a laugh, and Jemma gave her a knowing look as she nodded her head. "Well, nobody else in this room is flirting with him, so somebody has to stroke his ego."

Oh, if Jemma wasn't lying in a hospital bed at the moment . . . Taryn was certain her face glowed red enough to put any Christmas tree to shame.

Justin simply laughed. "No need to flirt, and my ego is just fine. I promise. It's payment enough to see you smile."

"Well, aren't you just a giant cliché." Jemma reached up and tweaked his ear, then sat back and eyed the bag in her lap. "There's something else in here."

"Oh, yeah." Justin reached over and rattled the bag toward him, then dipped inside and held something out to Taryn. "If I'm remembering right, this was your movie snack of choice."

Taryn leaned forward and grasped the blue tube of cookie dough, Justin's fingers brushing hers and telegraphing straight to her stomach. The fluttering anticipation there had nothing to do with sweet treats. "Thank you."

The soft words brought a look into Justin's eyes, holding Taryn closer than an embrace. "Anytime."

It was a look she hadn't seen in twelve years, and one she had never expected to see again. Her stomach accelerated from flutters, past butterflies, to full on red-tailed hawks.

"You're staying to watch the movie, right?" Jemma's voice intervened, breaking Justin's gaze and letting Taryn sink back into her chair.

"I wish I could." Reluctance coated the words like snow on Brown Mountain. "But I have to help Dad with some things tonight." Justin stood and pressed a kiss to the top of Jemma's head, then paused to look down at Taryn. "Meet me at Jemma's after church tomorrow. Dress warm." He was gone before she could answer.

His departure seemed to take her spine with him. She sank deeper against the chair, her eyes slipping closed. That kind of request should set any girl's heart on fire. Instead, the flames sizzled under cold fear.

12

Wind and mud stung Taryn's face and smeared her goggles. Her red knitted scarf flew out behind her, occasionally flipping back to flick her in the cheek. Justin's off-key, off-beat rendition of their old standby "Fishin' in the Dark" flew over his head, bounced off her helmet, and danced away on the wind.

She'd grin and maybe even sing along if it didn't mean there'd be mud in her teeth by the time they reached the first chorus.

When Justin said they should go get Jemma's traditional live Christmas tree from the firs planted at the far end of the orchard a couple of miles away, Taryn thought they'd be taking his truck.

Nope. He dug out the old four-wheeler from the barn, managed to get the thing running, tossed her a helmet, and told her to hold on.

With a bounce that nearly pitched her off the seat and over his head, he crashed through another mud puddle, breaking the thin sheen of ice glazing the top and shooting muddy water in all directions.

He had to be hitting those things on purpose.

Taryn swiped at her goggles with one hand, smearing the mud thin enough to see through more than actually removing it, then reached around and tightened her grip around Justin's waist as another giant puddle appeared on the path. Yep, he was definitely doing it on purpose.

And no, she did not notice how tight his abs were under his work jacket, which was also caked with damp mud. In spite of the look between them the night before, Taryn felt more relaxed than she had in more than a week. It had been too long since she'd let herself go in her beloved outdoors. School and Jemma and the quilt kept her indoors. The weather hadn't helped, what with the relative warmth finally giving way to winter chill mixed with rain and damp snow.

The two of them were bound to be a sight. A muddy, wet, laughing sight. Somebody was likely to call the press and tell them a two-headed Sasquatch had been spotted in the hills above Hollings.

With a whoop, Justin skidded sideways to a stop at the end of the orchard where the apple trees ended and the Fraser firs began. Years ago, Taryn's great-great-great-grandfather carved the orchard out of the forest on the hill above Hollings, but he left a couple of acres of the natural trees to flourish. Every Christmas, they came out, took down one tree, and replaced it with a seedling.

Taryn twisted around to find the tiny tree that Jemma bought two weeks ago still anchored to the small metal bracket behind her seat. Honestly. How did it survive Justin's driving?

He revved the engine, looking to the left and to the right. "Which way?"

"No way. Can I drive now?" She wasn't scared so much as sure there was already mud caked in her eyebrows, and it would never come out.

Justin turned to look over his shoulder, nose bare inches from hers. It was enough to steal her breath. He hadn't been this deep in her personal space since . . . well, in a long time. It tweaked her heart into a triple beat, almost making her wonder whether she didn't belong in the hospital right beside Jemma.

"Scared?" Justin's voice didn't sound quite right, maybe even a little strained. Probably the wind had dried out his throat.

Scared? Yes. Yes, she was. Because she had just become aware of the fact her arms were still tight around his waist and her chest was pressed up against his back. He probably thought she was making a move on him. Again. For the sake of what was a new beginning of their friendship, she loosened her grip and moved to sit back.

Justin gunned the engine and spun the tires off again. "Left it is!" His voice was carried away on the wind, and the speed forced Taryn to jerk her arms forward and hold on for all she was worth. Her heart forgot what just passed between them and decided it was okay to pull him close if it meant saving her life.

He slowed a couple of minutes later, the trees growing too thick for his breakneck speed. He tilted his head to the side and called over his shoulder, "Keep an eye open for the perfect tree. No Charlie Browns this year. Jemma deserves the biggest we can find."

Which reminded her . . . "Hey, genius. How are you planning to get the tree out of here once we find it? And how are you planning to cut it down?"

"I'll bring the truck back later. We'll mark the one you want. It was just easier this way." He gunned the engine. "And more fun."

Taryn sat back a little and let her hands rest on his waist, gripping his coat to keep some space between them. With the breakneck speed decreased to a slow crawl, her heart went back to the "he's so close" beat. "Easier? Nope. You just wanted to drive the quad. Just like when we were kids."

"Actually? I thought you could use some fresh air. You're working too hard, trying to be everything to everybody. It was making you tense."

There he went again, looking after her when she wasn't even sure she wanted him to. "Thanks."

He grinned over his shoulder at her and tapped the front of his helmet, then glided to a stop in the middle of a small clearing where several smaller trees surrounded them. The damp chill in the air hung heavy with the scent of evergreens and the expectation of snow. With the engine silenced, the quiet took control.

Pulling the helmet from his head, Justin sat back a little in his seat. "I haven't been back here in years."

"Probably not since the last time you came out here with Jemma and me to get a tree." Taryn pulled her own helmet off and finger combed her hair, wishing she'd brought a baseball cap.

He nodded, then slid off the four-wheeler. "The year your grandfather died. I was invited to be the man of the party and rock the chainsaw." He burned a few riffs on an air guitar.

"Good way to lose fingers if you're handling a chainsaw like you're in a rock band."

Justin held up his hand with his ring and middle fingers bent down, frowned, then gave Taryn a sheepish grin. With a shake of his hand, his fingers "magically" reappeared, then he swept his arms wide. "Find us a tree, m'lady. It's getting cold out here, and I want to come back with the truck before it gets too dark to find this spot again."

It didn't feel like so many Christmases had passed since her grandfather had died and Justin had made the trek out here with Jemma and Taryn and Fred the pickup. In the moment, watching Justin run his hands along tree branches as he analyzed how many needles fell, it seemed like just last week. One of those carefree, crazy days, one of the first times when she felt truly happy after the aneurysm jerked Grampa out of their lives forever.

Jemma had laughed at Justin's antics until tears ran down her face, good tears for the first time in a long time. She'd vowed to always bring him to "man up" with the chainsaw, even though she was perfectly capable of wrestling a tree down all by herself.

It was the first and last time Justin made the journey with them. The next year, he was in the army and Taryn was at college, wearing baggier sweaters every day and crying into her pillow every night.

"What's the frown all about?"

The nearness of his voice, right over her shoulder, pulled a huge, cold, stinging breath into her lungs. "Don't sneak up on me!" The words were snappier than she'd meant them to be, high on adrenaline and whatever else seemed to spike whenever he got too close. Apparently, her muscle memory of him was way too keen. She pulled in a calmer breath. "Just thinking about Grampa and Christmas and Jemma." It wasn't a lie. It just wasn't the whole truth.

"Well, turn your frown upside down."

Even if she didn't want to smile, there was no way she could stop it. "You may have a soldier's body, but there's a band geek still alive inside you."

He tipped his chin, then flexed an arm and tweaked his own bicep. "You think I have a soldier's body?"

Great. Now he knew she'd noticed.

Before she could turn red enough to melt the few flakes of snow already drifting down, he stepped around her and looked to the top of the tree she was standing beside. "I think you've found the perfect tree without even trying."

Taryn took a step back and eyeballed the branches. The girth was about right, just large enough to fill the space in front of the picture window without getting too close to the fireplace. "Think it's the right height?"

Justin ducked down to look at the trunk. "If it's not," his voice strained as he straightened, "there's enough play in the trunk for me to take it down a few inches, but it's looking good to my eye." He stepped back until he was shoulder to shoulder with her. "I think you've found what you need without having to look any farther."

It sounded like a loaded statement. Taryn watched him. He was busy gauging the tree, double-checking the size while she studied his profile and maybe started to hyperventilate just a little. What if beside her was everything she needed and her eighteen-year-old self manipulated it right out of her life?

"You're thinking again." He didn't even look at her. He just knew.

"About what I want for Christmas." She cleared her throat against the tightness threatening to swallow her. "Got to get my request in before it's too late, you know."

"And what did you decide you want? And it has to be something I can buy."

Nice, effective way to cut off the cop-out of Jemma being all better. "Fred." Where did that come from? Taryn hadn't thought of the truck in years until Justin showed up, but something deep inside her suddenly missed the old faithful pickup that disappeared with the last of her carefree self. With Justin around, she missed the girl who rattled around in a beat-up pickup singing old country songs with the life-long best friend who'd eased himself into being her one and only.

"Fred? Hm." He had a deep look on his face again.

It was a look she needed to wipe away. "What about you? What's on your Christmas list?"

"Legos." He fired a grin at her and tested the pine needles to make sure not too many pulled off. None did.

"You're kidding."

He shrugged. "Why not? There's not a lot you can't build with Legos."

"If you're twelve."

"I'm an eternal child at heart."

Okay, then. "So, Little Man Child, I'm wondering how you plan to mark this tree so you remember it when you come back."

"I won't forget."

"So you say now." She swept her arm in front of her. "There are more lookalikes here than you think there are."

He looked sideways at her, and his eyes dropped to her neck. "If you're so worried about my memory, you've got the perfect marker."

"You want me to stand out here and point at it and freeze my rear end off waiting for you to come back?"

"Your scarf, McKenna." He stepped between her and the tree and untied her scarf from its knot at the side of her neck. His fingers brushed her jaw line, catching her next breath. She was right. Being around him was dangerous. Too much of her heart still remembered how she used to feel about him, how much more they shared than he even realized.

She was so deep in her emotions it took a second to realize his fingers had stopped moving and he was staring her straight in the eye.

He looked exactly like she felt. He let his thumb drag across her jaw again, looking for something in her eyes, like he wasn't quite sure what it was he was looking for. "Know what I really want for Christmas?"

Her voice choked in her throat, refusing to come out. She shook her head, no longer caring what she wanted . . . what she was about to get . . . was something she shouldn't have.

The chorus of "White Christmas" blasted between them, dropping his hand and stealing the warmth from the moment, letting the ever-increasing chill intrude between them. "My cell phone." She took a step back. "I should get it. It might be Jemma."

Justin swallowed hard, nodded, and backed away, his face a mix of concern and disappointment.

Before she could even get the phone all the way to her ear, Rachel's voice came through. "Taryn?"

"I'm here. What's up?" Her voice sounded like she'd strangled on egg nog. It refused to clear.

"Are you okay?"

As a matter of fact, no, she wasn't. She watched Justin pull a red strip of plastic from his pocket and drape it over a tree limb. Taryn pulled at the end of her scarf and swallowed disappointment. Guess he didn't need it after all. Or maybe he didn't want it after all?

"Taryn?"

"I'm sorry, Rach." Turning her back on Justin, she took a few steps away and leaned back against the seat of the ATV. "I'm fine. Are you okay?" For the first time, alarm bells tripped. Rachel's voice sounded just as strained as her own.

"Jemma's fine, but you probably want to come up here. She's going stir-crazy. Like off her rocker stir-crazy, and she won't listen to reason."

Taryn sank deeper into the seat and glanced at her watch. It was nearly 3:30. Rachel was right. She should get back. Here she was, gallivanting around like everything was hunky-dory while Jemma lay up in the hospital with nowhere to go. "I'll be there in less than an hour. Do you need anything?"

"Tranquilizers."

"For you or for Jemma?"

"Maybe both. Are you at Jemma's by chance?"

"I am."

"Would you look in the freezer? Jemma froze some chicken and rice soup. Do you mind heating some up and putting it in the thermos in the cabinet under the microwave?"

"Will do."

"You can have some too." Rachel chuckled.

Taryn almost gagged. Ever since she was a kid and came down with a stomach bug after some of Jemma's county-famous chicken and rice soup, she couldn't even stand to smell the stuff. "You know not. It's bad enough I have to smell it heating up."

"I know. I'll see you in a few." Rachel clicked off the line without a good-bye.

"Jemma?" Justin crunched up behind her in the fresh snow.

"Rachel. Jemma's craving some of her own cooking and generally being Jemma." It took a second to face him after what had almost happened, but she turned and prayed they hadn't broken the friendship just as it was being restored.

"Can't say I blame her." He threw a leg over the quad. "Your chariot? I'll take you back, then come back to get the tree. If you leave the back door unlocked, I'll drop it off and lock up behind me."

Taryn climbed on and laid her hands at his waist, too scared of reigniting something she couldn't put out if she got too close to him again. "Thanks. Again."

"Anything for you, McKenna." He gunned the engine and took off, though the pace was much slower on the return trip.

13

Taryn rode the elevator to Jemma's floor alone, sipping on a surprisingly rich cup of hospital coffee. If she'd known it was this good, she would have stopped campaigning for a coffee shop in Hollings years ago. Guess somebody somewhere decided to pity the poor folks sitting up with loved ones and at least give them good caffeine.

When she rounded the corner on Jemma's floor, Rachel was in the hallway tapping her forehead against the wall. Taryn stopped for a second to watch. Either Jemma had gotten worse, or Rachel needed a psych doctor on the fourth floor. The behavior wasn't unfamiliar. Rachel had done this before, when one of her counselees positively refused to surrender to common sense. Jemma must be feeling better and bossing the doctors around, definitely a good sign.

"Rachel?"

Rachel brushed soft blonde hair out of her face and tucked it behind her ear, glanced sideways at Taryn, then went back to "banging" her head against the beige wall.

Taryn stopped about four feet away, just out of reach. "I'm not coming any closer until you tell me what's set you off. You scare me."

Forehead against the wall, Rachel sighed, gaze on the floor, curtain of gorgeous hair hiding her face. "Yeah, I scare me too." She lifted an arm listlessly and aimed a finger at the door to Jemma's room. "See for yourself. It's like herding a preschool class through a field trip at the zoo when the monkeys have just gotten loose. If there are less stressful things than a bored Jemma, can you please tell me what they are?"

Taryn patted the top of her head and pushed open the door to Jemma's room, stopping so short her coffee almost splattered all over the floor. "What are you *doing*?"

"See?" Rachel's voice floated in from the hallway.

Jemma was up, wearing the red satin pajamas Taryn had sent her after an Easter break missions trip to Cambodia.

Then again, to say Jemma was "up" would be wrong. She was on her knees, hooked up to her IV and monitors, dusting the baseboards. She looked over her shoulder at Taryn, rump up in the air.

Taryn pounded her free hand against her forehead and sank to the edge of the bed. "Jemma? The baseboards aren't clean enough for you? Do you know what will happen if your doctor comes in here and sees this or if, heaven forbid, the incredibly by-the-book nurse you had yesterday pops in here and catches you?"

Jemma turned and settled herself on the floor on her bottom. "Look at my face, Taryn. Do I care what they think? They need to just let me go home. I'm not going to die here like an old lady."

Taryn shook her head and hazarded a sip of coffee, not quite sure what else to do. Long ago, she'd learned not to try to boss Jemma around. It was the only reason she hadn't yanked her grandmother off the floor and tucked her back into bed. Jemma was like a child sometimes and needed to think something was her own idea before she'd cooperate.

It was ironic one of her grandmother's biggest fears in life was losing her sanity. Seemed like the years only sharpened her memory while they honed the razor's edge of her stubbornness. With behavior like this, it was a wonder they hadn't tested her for dementia. They might if they caught her cleaning baseboards with a spare toothbrush.

"Besides." Jemma held up her good hand and Taryn set her coffee down, then hauled her grandmother to her feet, careful not to snag the IV line on anything. Jemma took a moment to steady herself on her feet, then settled into the chair by the window. "There's a ton of dust around there. How am I supposed to get better if they give me a lung infection?"

"You're not going to get a lung infection." Taryn sat back on the bed and let her feet dangle as she scanned the baseboards. "And there's not any dust there."

Jemma dropped the toothbrush into the trash can by her chair. "Because I cleaned everything."

"You are so lucky I love you."

Taryn sighed, and when she opened her eyes, Jemma was smiling. The imp knew exactly what she'd done. "I know, sweetie."

"Rachel might not love you so much anymore. How many times did she tell you to stop?"

Jemma waved her hand toward the door in a gesture of dismissal. "Oh, she'll get over it."

"She's out there beating her head against the wall."

"She'll stop when she gets a good enough headache. And then she can have one of the aspirin I keep in my purse."

Taryn rolled her eyes. Time for a change of subject. "Has the doctor been in today?"

"He'll be around soon. I'm going to tell him it's time to let me go home."

"He'll let you go home when he's ready."

Jemma shook her head. "I'm pretty sure he can't keep me here if I don't want to be here."

"And I'm pretty sure your family gets a say so too."

"You think so?" With a flick of her free wrist, she pulled and straightened the sleeve of her pajamas. "Is Rachel coming back in before she leaves?"

Rachel's purse sat on the floor by Jemma's chair. "I'm guessing yes. And you'd better behave when she does." Sliding her feet to the floor, Taryn crossed to Jemma and knelt beside her, careful to set her cup on the table so she didn't dump it all over the freshly cleaned floor. "You have to listen to the doctor, Old Woman," Taryn teased gently with the nickname she gave her stubborn grandmother years before.

Jemma smiled as Taryn stood. "I should. But I don't have to."

"This is true." Taryn patted her grandmother's knee and looked down at her, hoping it would buy her some sort of illusion of authority. "But Rachel and I and a whole lot of other people would like to have you around for a while. You can live a million more years, but you've got to take care of yourself."

"And is it living if all the most physical movement I can have is lifting the remote off the end table and changing the channel between *Wheel of Fortune* and *Jeopardy*?" She was getting angry. It was evident on the portable heart monitor attached to her IV pole. Plus, Taryn knew what Jemma's angry looked like. It was quiet and clipped. And it didn't get much quieter or more clipped than this. "I'll have you know, young lady, I took care of myself before you were born, and I can take care of myself now."

"And I'll have you know it was thirty years since I was born. Time's passed, Jem."

She huffed a breath and looked away. "I'm not going into seclusion, Taryn."

"Nobody asked you to. But I'll bet if you agree to some of the doctor's conditions, he'll let you go home a lot sooner."

"Which conditions?" Jemma was finally ready to negotiate.

"No hiking around the field. No climbing up to the roof. Definitely no rickety old wooden stepladders." Taryn tipped her head toward the wall behind her. "And absolutely no scrubbing floors on your hands and knees, okay? I'm surprised the nurses didn't head in here to see why your heart monitor was going wacky."

"They probably headed this way and got distracted by your cousin and her head injury in the hallway."

The laughter couldn't be helped. Jemma would be the death of her someday.

Jemma cracked a smile. "Will you check and make sure she hasn't given herself a concussion? I promise not to clean anything else while you're gone."

The coffee sloshed in the cup as Taryn stepped toward the door, muttering, "I'm surprised you haven't been diagnosed with OCD."

"I heard you. My old ears are better than you think."

Taryn stepped into the hallway, the door creaking lightly behind her.

Rachel stood leaning against the wall, eyes staring blankly at a framed photo across the hall.

Taryn leaned next to her cousin and held the cup of coffee in front of her nose. "Have some. It's surprisingly good."

The scent of cooling coffee must have worked because Rachel gripped the cup and took a sip. Her eyebrows went up. "You got this here?"

"Mmm hmm."

She took a longer sip. "Hm. Who knew?"

"Best-kept secret in town, apparently. Wonder if the food's good?"

"Could be Mark's and my new date spot." The words were meant to be funny, but her voice was too dull to lift a smile from either one of them.

She tried to pass the cup back, but Taryn shoved her hand away. "Keep it. You look like you need it more than I do."

"Thanks."

"Want to talk about it?"

Rachel was silent, cup useless in her hands, eyes still focused on the pastels across the hall.

"Rachel, talk to me. Jemma couldn't have been frustrating enough to make you mute."

Fabric scraped against the wall as Rachel almost doubled over. It was like Taryn had a front-row seat to the collapse of her emotions.

"I just don't think this is going to end well. And today was the first time I got a good idea about it."

"It'll be fine." The words came out even though Taryn didn't mean them. She hoped they sounded more convincing to Rachel than to herself.

"No. And don't play Little Pollyanna to me." The coffee cup rolled back and forth between Rachel's palms. "You heard the list of restrictions, and you saw her in the room today cleaning as hard as she could go. She didn't clean those baseboards because she's got a dust vendetta. She did it to show the doctors and the nurses they can't tell her what to do. She'll keep right on doing everything exactly like she's always done and, one day, she'll drop dead right in the middle of the back orchard. You watch." She finally looked at Taryn. "And you'll be the one to find her."

Her words were like a fist to Taryn's diaphragm. It was like the time she fell off a friend's trampoline in elementary school and landed flat on her back, knocking all of the air out of her lungs, the blow so hard she couldn't inhale for what felt like forever. It was the same panicked, gasping pain.

Rachel sighed. "You hadn't thought about it."

Taryn shook her head, caught up in flashing images not fully formed, of her grandmother prone, helpless, and dying. It was like the worst nightmare ever, only there was no waking up from this one.

Rachel tapped Taryn's cheek with the side of the coffee cup. "Here. Now I think you need this more than I do."

───※───

The screen door slammed behind Taryn, smacking her in the rear end and knocking her two steps forward. Yep. It felt more like a Monday than a Wednesday, and getting hit in the rear was a fitting end to the day. All day, she'd dragged six steps behind herself, exhausted from the emotions and too many nights of restless sleep. Her mind was muddled alphabet soup, jumbled with no coherent meaning.

To boot, Jemma had been an absolute bear at the hospital. All she wanted was to come home, but the doctor insisted on two more days. They'd had to up her clot-busting drugs again, and this time the medication seemed to be working. The timing was perfect for Taryn because Friday was the first day of her Christmas break from school, but it was making Jemma downright cranky. Taryn hadn't been in the room fifteen minutes before her grandmother decided she was better off alone.

Taryn was frustrated, but her feelings were unimportant in the face of what Jemma was going through. She had swallowed her hurt at being kicked out, kissed Jemma on the forehead, and left, telling herself she was grateful for the extra time at home.

Extra time at home. Taryn let her backpack slip to the floor in front of the fridge, dropped mail bloated by Christmas cards on the counter, and headed straight for the den. She'd crank up the fireplace and lie down on the couch. Maybe she'd be tired enough to actually fall asleep.

At the doorway to the den, her feet dragged to a stop. Rachel's nearly finished quilt lay draped across the back of her couch. If Jemma was coming home on Friday, she had two days to finish the quilt. So long early bedtime.

Pulling in a deep breath, she abandoned the idea of a nap, letting it go with a sigh, and flopped onto the couch next to the quilt, allowing her hand to run down the fabric. It was probably her imagination, but it seemed to release the faint scent of Justin, all woodsy outdoors and fresh soap. His presence lingered, almost like he was sitting there beside her, easing his way back into her life.

Taryn let her eyes close and dropped her head back to the couch. For the past two nights, he'd shown up on her doorstep after she got home from visiting Jemma, always with food, always laughing and talking and stitching like nothing had ever happened between them. Not once had he brought up what had almost happened in the woods on Sunday. Not once had he talked about the past. Everything was focused on the now with him. It almost seemed like he took pleasure in being with her doing something as un-Justin as sewing fabric squares into strips and strips into the body of the quilt.

Stupid quilt. If Jemma hadn't decided to take on a tradition not her own, if the first quilt hadn't been ruined, if Justin wasn't so insistent on helping her . . . they'd have never spent all of this time together. He wouldn't have nearly kissed her. She wouldn't have wanted him to.

Marnie's words wouldn't be chasing around in her head, keeping her awake more than Jemma's illness ever could. *I meant the line about love finding you when you least expect it. You certainly weren't expecting Justin back.*

No, she wasn't. Taryn had always secretly missed him, but she sure hadn't expected to see him in her life again. Not this close. She leaned forward and propped her elbows on her knees, staring at the floor. This was all moving so fast. Two weeks ago, she hadn't seen Justin in a dozen years. Now she was starting to forget the time had passed, was starting to think she wanted so much more than the friendship she'd caved in to.

The sooner they finished the quilt, the better. Then he wouldn't have any reason to keep coming around, and they could each go on with their lives, separately, friends bumping into one another occasionally, like it should have been all along. He'd never have to know what she'd done and could go on without the burden of knowing Sarah was out there.

There was only an hour or two of work left on the stitching, and the quilt would be done. Taryn glanced at the clock. If she started now, it would be nearly finished if Justin showed up as he had the past few nights. She could tell him good-bye, and it would be for the last time.

But she couldn't make her fingers pick up the quilting hoop she'd finally resorted to using when they started stitching rows together. The thought of it made her fingers ache. The thought of doing it without Justin present made her heart ache worse. She'd wait. Give herself one more evening with him before she shut the door behind him and went back to regular life.

The thought depressed her, but it had to be done. What she needed was to sip a good, hot cup of her mom's Russian tea and to open her Christmas cards.

In short order, she had the fireplace going and had settled into the recliner with the warm citrus scent of tea drifting from an end table and the mail on her lap. She flipped through the seven or eight envelopes, noting return addresses, mostly people from church, a couple from college friends, and one or two from distant relatives. The last one was different, not a card but a letter in a plain envelope, the handwriting familiar, the return address from Texas.

Sarah.

The girl usually tucked notes in with letters or cards from her mom once or twice a year. Never had she gone to the trouble to write on her own. Taryn's heart picked up speed until she thought it would bounce out of her chest and high-tail it for safety under the couch across the room.

Breaking the envelope seal, Taryn pulled out the folded notebook paper gently, as if it was fragile enough to crumble in her hands, and unfolded it. Sarah's handwriting curled across the page, impossibly neat for a middle schooler's, nothing like Taryn's own.

Aunt Taryn,

For the first time, it feels weird to call you that. I sort of want to write Mom Taryn or Mama McKenna, which sounds kind of cool, but I don't know if you'd like it.

I've been talking to Mom and Dad a lot lately about you. See, I know they love me and I'm glad they're my parents, but sometimes it's not enough. Sometimes I wonder who I am and how much of me is like you. Mom says these are big questions for a kid. She said it makes me sound like an old soul. I guess I just think about it a lot.

She said one time you wouldn't come to see me unless I asked you myself. So here's me asking you myself. Will you come see me? Maybe for my birthday? Mom and Dad said it's okay, and I'd like it. A lot.

Love,
Sarah Josephs

Taryn didn't even realize she was crying until a tear splotched the middle of *birthday*. The edges of the paper crumpled in her grip. What could she do? To get on a plane and fly to Texas and see what she'd lost would rip her apart.

To say no would be to abandon Sarah fully, to leave that little girl feeling just like Taryn's dad had left her to feel.

To go would mean she had to tell Justin the truth because it would be the height of wrong to look their daughter in the eye without him.

Their daughter.

Taryn dropped the letter to her lap, buried her face in her hands, and cried.

14

"Child, you have not stopped chattering since they settled me into the blessed wheelchair in the hospital, and you finally believed they were letting me come home." Jemma was aiming for her stern voice, but she missed. The slight tilt of her lips was a dead giveaway she was anything but mad. If she were to get down to being honest, she was just as excited as Taryn, who was bouncing and chattering in the backseat.

Christmas was six days away, and Jemma was headed home. Taryn didn't care if it was the only present she received for the next decade.

Justin met her eye in the rearview mirror, shook his head, and smiled a crooked smile. She sat back against the leather rear seat of his pickup, heart pounding hard enough to require a trip right back to the hospital. He shouldn't smile at her. It only reinforced what she was realizing she wanted badly but couldn't have. It twisted the decision about Sarah into a knot in her gut, bringing a deeper ache than she'd ever felt before.

A frown drew her eyebrows together when her attention went back to Jemma. Justin and Sarah were things to think about late at night, when she was home trying to fall asleep, unable to because he was slowly tangling himself back into her heart.

Right now, nothing could be allowed to bring her down. Jemma was coming home in time for Christmas. *Thank you, Lord.* He'd answered this prayer, but it created an uneasy twinge around her heart. Things just couldn't stay good for long. They never did.

"You drive slower than my great-grandmother." Jemma goaded Justin from the front seat beside him. He'd been easing around the dips in the dirt driveway leading to the farmhouse, going at a turtle's pace, and Jemma had just about had enough.

Taryn knew what was on her grandmother's mind. She wanted to make sure the house had fared well in the nearly two weeks she'd been gone.

And she should be wanting to make sure. Her grand-daughter was not known for her excessively awesome cleaning skills. Those definitely got left in the gene pool when Taryn climbed out and toweled off.

"You just got out of the hospital. Last thing I need is your granddaughter screaming in my ear because I bounced the stuffing out of you on this driveway." Justin flashed Taryn another look. "You know how she can be."

Taryn slapped him in the back of the head, which only elicited a chuckle from him and a knowing look from Jemma.

Jemma could smile like the Cheshire Cat all she wanted. It had become clear to Taryn she'd have to hold Justin to acquaintance level, no matter how much it hurt, and her grandmother would have to be content with it. They'd have to sit down and talk after Justin left. Jemma could not be playing matchmaker, no matter what her motives, not with all the things Taryn couldn't say.

The truck didn't speed up one iota, even though Jemma leaned forward and fried Justin with her impatient glare.

He kept his eyes out the windshield in front of him, where the wipers swept away a spitting snow flurry. "When was the last time you had the driveway graded?"

Jemma shrugged. "I have no idea. I usually don't notice it's uneven."

Taryn snorted. "Because you drive up here at eighty and go airborne every time you hit a bump."

The look she shot over her shoulder should have left Taryn gasping for breath, but all she got in return was a smile. Taryn refused to be scared today. Jemma was coming home, albeit with restrictions she may or may not follow. Any discussion would have to wait until later.

Taryn couldn't wait until her grandmother saw the tree in the den and the quilt laid out on the table. It might not be the one she had planned, but she'd be doing back flips over the fact Rachel would have a quilt for her wedding. It had yet to be backed, but she'd already talked to Holly and would carry it into Dalton on Monday to have it machine-quilted to the backing. The hard part was done.

"Tell you what," Justin rounded the back of the house and slowed to a stop by the back door behind Jemma's Blazer. "After Christmas, I'll borrow the tractor from Dad and come over and smooth out some of these holes for you. I'm afraid if it doesn't get done soon, the thawing and freezing of all the rain and damp we've had so far will do nothing but make the whole thing worse."

Justin was coming back? Even though the roof was repaired and the quilt his misplaced guilt had driven him to help with was finished? Even though Jemma was back home and he could safely walk away now?

He was eyeballing Taryn in the mirror again, but this time, it looked like he was trying to read her more than say anything. When he realized she was looking at him, he smiled a smile that didn't quite reach his eyes, then popped the door open and looked at Jemma. "I'll come around and help you out."

"Like fun you will." Jemma had the door open and was out of the truck before Justin could even get around the front fender.

He shrugged and pulled Taryn's door open for her. "You okay?"

"Perfectly fine." For the most part.

Shutting the door, he walked around the back of the truck beside her. "You staying with Jemma tonight?"

"Your guess is as good as mine. I should, but she probably won't let me." No matter what the doctor said, no matter what Taryn wanted, it was pretty much a guarantee her grandmother would boot her out of the house right after *Wheel of Fortune*, telling her she was perfectly capable of taking care of herself. This in spite of the fact Jemma was not left-handed, and the doctor told her not to do anything more strenuous than walk from the den to the bedroom.

The woman would be making gingersnap cookies within two hours of being in the back door. After all, she was behind on her Christmas baking.

"Hey." Justin grabbed Taryn's wrist before they could get all the way around the truck. "Since there's no sewing and no decorating to be done tonight, I was going to see if—"

"Taryn, do you have your key?" Jemma stood at the top of the concrete steps, holding the white wooden screen door open with her shoulder while she tried to rummage through her purse one-handed. "Mine's not in my purse. It's probably still hanging on the rack by the door."

Turning away from Justin, Taryn dug into her pocket. It was way better not to know where his sentence was going.

By the time the door was unlocked and Jemma was kicking her shoes off inside as she leaned against the washing machine, Justin was at Taryn's shoulder. "You excited about what she's going to say?"

A grin was the only answer Taryn had. Definitely. It was the first time she'd ever felt like she was able to pay Jemma back in some way for all she'd done for her.

Jemma settled her shoes under the hooks and shrugged out of her coat, struggling with the left arm.

Justin moved to step around Taryn and help, but she held up a hand to stop him.

Jemma would rather struggle for ten minutes and do it herself than accept help from one of them. She finally sandwiched the hem of the sleeve between her fingertips and the cast and managed to slip her arm out. The smug look she gave Taryn and Justin set them firmly in their places. "Know what I could use?" She was off, into the kitchen before either Justin or Taryn could even slip out of their coats. "A nice cup of coffee."

"Decaf," Taryn called, tossing her coat and hoping it caught on a hook. "And I'll make it for you."

"Honestly, child. Filling the coffeepot is not going to send me into cardiac arrest." Jemma huffed her frustration as she pulled the carafe from the coffee maker. "There is such a thing as too much help. And hovering. You are definitely hovering." She planted the carafe against Taryn's stomach and gently eased her back a couple of feet. "There. I can breathe now."

Taryn flared her nostrils, knowing better than to take offense. The queen of England would get the same treatment if she showed up and tried to help. Far from being insulted, it did her heart good to see Jemma was still her Jemma. A tiny part of Taryn had been afraid her grandmother would come home an old woman, one who shriveled up in her recliner until she wasted away into nothing. Seemed like the opposite had happened, and too much "rest" in the hospital had Jemma raring to go.

"You ought to know I'm not going to sit in there in front of the TV and wither away."

"Stop reading my mind." Taryn popped open the cabinet door and reached up to pull the decaf from its perch way in the back, then settled back onto her heels.

Justin leaned against the counter next to Taryn, arms crossed over his chest, watching the proceedings. "Yep, I was right. This is exactly where you get it." His voice was low and intimate. "Stubborn as the day is long."

The bag of coffee squeezed like a pillow between her fingers, releasing the warm smell of roasted comfort. "And don't you forget it."

She turned to hand the coffee to Jemma, but Justin grabbed her upper arm and tipped his head toward her, whispering, "She spotted the quilt."

Jemma had stopped stock-still, coffee carafe in the sink and hand on the faucet, staring over the bar at the kitchen table where the quilt was spread in all of its green-and-white glory. She was completely silent.

Taryn shot a glance over her shoulder at Justin, who straightened and stood so his chest hovered just out of reach of her back, the warmth of him filtering through her shirt and into her heart. It took all she had not to lean back into him, to give herself one moment where she could pretend there was something between them, and this could go where she'd always wished it could go, with no secret holding them apart like an invisible barrier.

"Taryn." Jemma dropped her hand from the faucet, leaving the water running, and gripped the edge of the counter. "What is this?"

Justin rested his hand at the small of Taryn's back and urged her forward.

She glanced back to catch his grin. They'd rendered Jemma close to speechless. It was a nearly impossible feat.

There was a high five in his eyes. *Good job us. Way to go, team.*

"It's Rachel's quilt. For her wedding. Justin and I finished it for you."

Jemma had yet to take her eyes off the quilt. Rounding the bar, she reached out a finger but stopped just short of touching the fabric. "This is not Rachel's quilt."

"I know." Leaving Justin behind in the kitchen and stepping around the bar, Taryn slipped up behind her grandmother and laid a hand on her shoulder. "But it's hand-sewn just like you wanted. I didn't want to tell you while you were in the hospital, but there was a leak and—"

"Where did you get this?" There was a tremor in her voice, one that dropped Taryn's hand from her shoulder and drove her back a step. Something was off, something not good.

"In the attic. I found it when we were bringing down the Christmas decorations, and since it was already half-sewn, it was the only way to get one done for Rachel in time for the wedding. There was no way, even with Justin's help, for me to get a new one cut and pieced in time after a leak ruined the first one. This one dropped into our lap and—"

"You and Justin sewed this together." It was not a question. And she still hadn't looked at Taryn. "Isn't this just fitting." Jemma's voice was laced with the tears hanging on her eyelashes. "If you two would have just waited, would have hung on, and waited like you should have, it would have been yours."

Taryn took a step back as a rustle came from the kitchen. "What would have been whose?"

"Your father. Your awful father. I never should have let him influence me, should have kept him away from you, talked some sense into you instead of listening to him." It was as if Jemma was alone in the room. She'd lost all focus save for the quilt. "He'd have asked you like he planned, and everything would be so much different."

The tone of her voice chilled Taryn. Straight from her heart, it made the hairs rise up on the back of her neck. "Who was going to ask me what?" But she already knew the answer. Deep inside, where she wouldn't even admit it, she already knew. Some sort of crazy nausea gripped her, and she pressed her fingers against her mouth, hard, letting her other hand press them even tighter.

Over the bar, her eyes met Justin's. He looked stricken, the set of his jaw hard. When he caught Taryn's eye, his mouth opened, then shut. His eyes flickered away and back again, unreadable.

Behind her, Jemma kept talking. "I should have let you tell him instead of letting your father convince me it was for the best for you to give the baby away."

Jemma, no. Taryn's heart beat twice on a surge of adrenaline. It gripped her chest and shot pain to her fingertips. Her head swung back and forth. *No. No. No.*

Everything about Justin froze. Everything. He didn't even blink.

Maybe Taryn was lucky, and someone stopped time in the instant before those words hit his ears.

But then his hands came up between them and, if it were possible, he stood even taller. His chin dipped slightly. "What baby?"

Jemma gasped. "Taryn . . ."

Taryn's head kept shaking back and forth, her fingers pressing tighter and tighter against her lips until it was impossible she wasn't tasting blood. The tears pounded at the back of her eyelids in rhythm with her heartbeat. *No. No. No. Not. Like. This.*

Justin's hands lowered and clenched into fists, pressing into his thighs. "Taryn." His voice was low and deep and wounded. "What baby?"

Words wouldn't even form in her head, even if they had, her jaw was too tight, her throat too full for them to squeeze out.

"That's why you vanished." His words were impossibly slow, dragged out and quiet.

"Justin." His name squeezed out around Taryn's fingers, weak and feeble.

He held his arm straighter, hand halting the rest of her words. He pressed his lips tight, shook his head, and walked out.

Taryn jumped and squeezed her eyes shut as the back door slammed, rattling the house and shaking her off the last fragile inch of her foundation.

—∞∞∞—

"Taryn." Jemma's voice broke through the roar in Taryn's ears. She grasped her granddaughter's wrist and pulled her hands away from her mouth. "Sit down." Reaching around, she patted Taryn's back, then pressed on her shoulder, easing her into the kitchen table chair that had somehow appeared right behind her.

Jemma pulled her own chair around and sat knee to knee with Taryn, waiting, just like she used to do when she was little and had a bad dream. Her grandmother would sit on the edge of the bed, pat Taryn's knee, and wait for her to talk.

Taryn couldn't look her in the eye. This was her homecoming, her moment of freedom after being in the hospital. It was supposed to be filled with fun surprises like the quilt and the tree in the living room, and quiet calm for her to recover. Taryn had wrecked it all. "I'm so sorry." Her voice was thin in the room, drowned out by the ticking clock passing seconds on the wall.

"For what?"

"This. Today. It wasn't supposed to be like this." Taryn waved a hand toward the den behind her. "We even got you a live tree. Justin and me."

"I'm sure it's beautiful. I can smell it from here. You two went out to the back side of the orchard, didn't you?" Jemma patted her granddaughter's knee and sat back. "Is that where you were on Sunday when you were so late coming to the hospital?"

"I'm sorry." Seemed there was an endless supply of things to apologize for.

"Stop." Jemma's smile was a flash before it disappeared. "My big old mouth. Taryn, I'm so sorry. I just . . . I forgot he was here."

Taryn hadn't. She couldn't. Not the way he'd looked at her. There was no way the image would ever go away.

"It was just the idea of you and Justin sewing the quilt with each other. The irony of it. You finding it right as he shows back up, and then you working on it together. It just . . ."

"What did you mean it was mine?" The truth was there, but she wanted to hear it from her grandmother.

Jemma shook her head and sat forward, forcing Taryn to look her in the eye. "Justin came to me just before the two of you graduated from high school. You'd only been dating a little over a year, but you'd been friends since the cradle. I knew exactly what he wanted when he showed up."

"Don't say it." Taryn sat back, not wanting to hear it out loud after all. It wasn't real, and nothing had been lost if nobody ever said it out loud.

"I told him he had my blessing a thousand times over. When the two of you fought and he didn't ask you . . . I used to wonder what would separate the two of you, but then you got pregnant, and it was obvious. I folded up the quilt and put it away. Probably I should have destroyed it, but I just couldn't do it."

Everything made sense now. The way Justin acted the day she begged him to stay, then tried to manipulate him to stay. The regret slumping his shoulders when he walked away from her. Taryn had blown it with her neediness. Her fault. All her fault. Always her fault.

"No wonder he thinks I vanished. Because I did. I pushed him away and then let him walk away." Taryn dropped her face into her hands. "I blew it. And now, I blew it again by not telling him. He'll never forgive me for this. And he shouldn't."

Jemma was so quiet it was as if she'd left the room, even though her knees were in full view between Taryn's fingers. Finally, she pulled in a deep, shuddering breath. "Honey, when he said you vanished, he didn't mean what you're thinking."

"What else could he mean?"

"I'll be right back." Her voice was so heavy, it was a wonder she could stand up, but she did, leaving Taryn to sit and catalog her mistakes.

This couldn't stay a secret forever. Taryn had always known it would come out eventually. Dropping her head back onto the chair, she stared at Jemma's ceiling and counted the dents from dozens of Happy New Year champagne pops when her grandparents used to get together with their best friends every December 31. They had a good life together, full of laughter, lots of love and acceptance and mutual respect.

There were some brief mumbling, a bang, and a rustle from Jemma's room, then she reappeared in the kitchen doorway, holding an envelope. Handing it to Taryn, she went to turn off the sink she'd left running when she first spotted the quilt.

It was one of those long white security envelopes, the edges worn like somebody had handled it often. It was sealed, one corner torn slightly. Taryn flipped it over to see the front. Maybe it was from her mother, something left behind for the moment her daughter needed it most. Now would definitely qualify as the time.

The front of the envelope sucked her breath away. It was Justin's handwriting, addressed to her. The postmark was one week after she'd left for college. Six weeks after they parted on his front lawn. Six weeks of her tears and her guilt and her condemnation over what she'd done to him. Right after she found out there was a baby coming into the world.

Taryn swallowed hard around a lump in her throat the size of one of the Brodigan apples in the orchard. "What is this?"

Not a sound came from Jemma in the kitchen. It was like she'd disappeared.

Standing and whipping around, Taryn held the envelope up beside her face, the paper shaking, crumpling in her clenched fist. "What is this?" Her voice climbed louder. It wouldn't be stopped, wouldn't tone down. As much guilt as had lain on her like a blanket half an hour ago, there was an equal amount of disbelief flaming now.

"It came right after you found out you were pregnant." There was a metallic clang as Jemma settled the teakettle on the stove. "You were already on your way to Pennsylvania. Your father called in the morning before the mail ran, and the conversation . . ." She stopped talking and gripped the handle of the oven, eyes fixed on the blue ceramic tile behind the stove. "It was full of every reason your mother never should have married him. All of those things about how she used you to hold on to him and to ruin his life, how all of his plans were wrecked because you were born because she wouldn't give you up like he said she should. He said she was selfish, clingy, needy."

The same things Justin had seen in Taryn.

It stung the back of Taryn's eyelids, even though there was nothing new being said. "All of the things he said about how he stayed here instead of taking a job in California . . ." The words rang in her father's voice in her head. But still . . . She gripped the envelope tighter, the corner poking her palm.

"I held onto the letter for a couple of days, thinking you were too emotional, and there was too much going on. And the longer I held it, the harder it was to give it to you." Jemma's knuckles were nearly white on the oven handle. "I thought about it a lot, but it was for the best."

For the best. The same words Jemma had said to Taryn when she encouraged her to give up the baby, to not tell Justin, to not tell anyone. The same words she'd used when she started to sound like Taryn's father, convincing her it was best not to ruin Justin's life, to let this go, to let someone who was happily married and desperate for a baby, in the position to properly care for one, have Sarah to raise.

"I watched your mother wither, Taryn. Your father, before they married, he was a wonderful man, one we would have been proud to call a son, always here helping your grandfather. But something snapped in him when your mother got pregnant." She cleared her throat, her voice straining around tears. "He said she did it on purpose to keep him from going to California. Maybe she did. I never had the courage to ask her. But I couldn't stand by and watch you make the same mistake. Sweet baby girl," her voice fell to a whisper, "you and your mother suffered so much with her married to a man who resented you both. I couldn't watch the same thing happen to you."

"So you manipulated the situation yourself." Why was her voice so low? She was furious, but she couldn't take it out on Jemma now, not when she'd just come home from the hospital. "You listened to *my father,* and you twisted the situation to end how *you* wanted. How *you* thought was best. You manipulated me. And Justin." *And our child.*

A car door shut softly outside. Taryn turned to watch the back door. Justin had come back? Already?

Jemma came around the bar and laid her hands on Taryn's shoulders. "You're angry. And you should be. Go home. I made a phone call. Marnie's here to stay with me tonight." She brushed the hair out of Taryn's face. "It's okay. I understand, but don't you dare stay here and hold all of this in."

Unable to argue, too scared to try, Taryn shoved the letter in her pocket and brushed by Jemma, out into the mud-room, then pulled her hiking boots on. Without looking back, she yanked her coat off the hook and slammed out the back door into the cold.

15

How could her own grandmother manipulate her? How could Jemma listen to Taryn's father, of all people, the man who had made her own daughter's life miserable for so long, who'd treated her granddaughter like a nuisance at best, a flat-out fly to be swatted away at worst?

Taryn had never, ever questioned Jemma. Never believed she was capable of anything other than sheer, bossy honesty to a fault. But now . . . it was like everything she knew about her grandmother blew up in her face. She'd lied for years by hiding the letter.

"How could you?" It felt good to shout it, to scream it at the top of her lungs, to let the words bounce off the walls of her small kitchen and back to her, even if Jemma couldn't hear them. The raw pain in Taryn's throat felt like relief so much she wanted to yell it again and again, to shout it until her voice grew ragged and she couldn't feel the hurt anymore.

But doing so would only bring nosy Mrs. Jenkins over to make sure no one was in the house trying to murder her.

Too late. Some part of Taryn had already died. After all, Rachel was wrapped up in Ethan and Mark. Justin was gone for good. Jemma was not who she'd always seemed to be. There was nothing left for Taryn to hold on to.

The stupid quilt. The stupid, stupid quilt. If she hadn't gotten into things none of her business in the attic . . . If Jemma hadn't been so dead set on making Rachel a quilt of her own . . . If Justin had fixed the leak instead of rushing her to the hospital with Jemma . . . Taryn and Jemma would be sitting in Jemma's den right now in blissful ignorance. The same cozy little family of two in front of the fireplace, probably drinking hot chocolate, eating the cookies Jemma had baked, and admiring the decorating they'd done before this whole nightmare started.

Those days seemed forever ago. Taryn could dream it all day, but the cozy little scene wasn't going to happen. None of this could go back and be undone.

Stupid quilt. Without it, life would be perfect. Taryn would never have known Justin was planning to ask her to marry him.

She'd have said yes. Her palms pressed tight against the cool vinyl of the refrigerator. The baby . . . Sarah . . . It would have been a shock, but it would have been a joy to bring a child into the world together, right?

Then again, if they'd gotten married, she'd have had to follow him wherever the army sent him, away from Jemma, away from the only family she knew, the only person who ever loved her without conditions.

Needy. Manipulative. You used me. Justin had said those words to her, standing in his front yard the day he left. And he was right. Marry him? They'd have been miserable. All of those things he'd said about her were true. Her mistake had saved him. Good thing he figured her out before it was too late.

Taryn ran one hand across her stomach. Well, almost before it was too late.

The letter crinkled in her pocket as her forearm brushed it. Two letters in one week, Sarah wanting to meet her face-to-face, Justin saying things she couldn't even begin to guess. Twelve years apart and both life-changing.

Not for the first time, Taryn doubted her decision. Too much new information had her head tied in knots. She walked into the living room to fire up her gas fireplace and sit cross-legged on the edge of the white brick hearth. Settling the letter on the floor in front of her, Taryn smoothed out the wrinkles and laid her palms flat against it. "I thought he hated me." Maybe he hadn't. Maybe her father and Jemma were wrong. Maybe she was wrong. Maybe Justin at eighteen was nothing at all like her father at eighteen.

"Oh, Lord." Her eyes drifted shut. She dropped her forehead against the letter. "What if I was wrong, God? What if I ruined both of our lives?" Taryn sniffed, feeling the tears pushing against the back of her eyes. "What if I ruined all three of our lives?"

It was the one place she never allowed her imagination to wander, but now the movie spun up in her mind. Sarah was eleven now, about to be twelve. Her letter was so grown-up, so wise to her situation. How different would this Christmas be, probably buying Sarah her first cell phone? Maybe, since Justin came home to be with his dad, picking out a house where they'd all settle in Hollings or Dalton?

Would she still be a teacher?

Keeping Sarah would have meant leaving school to follow Justin wherever the army sent him. For the first time, Taryn considered what it would have meant for her to sacrifice for the baby instead of for Justin. She'd always thought of it in terms of saving Justin from being tied to her like her father was tied to her mother, but was some part of her being selfish? Refusing to give up her dreams to raise their child?

"Did I do the right thing?" She couldn't even raise her face to look up, but God had to hear her. He had to.

If she'd given up college, she wouldn't be a teacher. Wouldn't be available to a kid like Chelsea who just needed someone to listen. There had been countless Chelseas in her life. Were they worth one of Sarah, when Sarah had the family she needed?

Did I do the right thing?

Not by lying to the adoption agency by telling them she didn't know who the father was. Not by lying to Justin by not telling him at all. He never got a say in what happened to his own daughter. The betrayal he had to be feeling . . .

Must be something like the betrayal Taryn was feeling, only worse.

She sat up and stared at the closed blinds of her front window. Milky winter sun bled in around the slats. Jemma and Taryn had the exact same motives, protecting the ones they loved. How could she stalk out on Jemma for the same thing she'd done herself?

The realization didn't make the anger die. It just dialed the heat down to a low simmer. Taryn might have lied, but Jemma manipulated the whole situation, and something in her just wasn't ready to let it go.

Not until she knew what past Justin had to say back then.

The morbid side of Taryn, the side whispering for her to slow down and rubberneck when she passed a police car or a fire truck, dragged out the suspense as long as possible.

The envelope was thin, too thin to be more than one sheet, and it had been handled. A lot.

She picked it up and let it lay on her fingers, splayed in the open space between her two hands. The edges were shiny with someone's repeated touch. Jemma didn't just tuck this away and hide it. She'd worried it, thought about it, likely agonized over it. Just like Taryn, in her tiny little off campus apartment, all those nights when she thought maybe, just maybe, she should call Justin, only to have his face crowded out by her father's scowl.

She'd done the right thing. Hadn't she?

Did Jemma lay awake at night and wonder whether she'd done the right thing too?

Finally, when her heart couldn't take any more, she slipped her index finger into the small tear in the corner and popped the seal, which was weak with a decade of time and touch.

The sheet of notebook paper was reluctant to let go of its folds, like it was not quite yet willing to tell her all she wanted to know.

She wanted to read it slowly, to take in what it said line by line, but her eyes wouldn't wait. They skimmed sentences.

> *I'm sorry.*
>
> *. . . my fault too.*
> *. . . never should have said what I said.*
> *. . . thought I wanted to marry you.*
> *Maybe we should wait.*
> *I still love you.*

Her nose wrinkled, tickled by tears. She dragged a finger across the last sentence. *I still love you.* In spite of her manipulating him into sleeping with her. In spite of her trying to hammer his dreams out of him. He sat on his cot in basic training and said he still loved her.

Broken her. Unworthy her. Lying, manipulating, needy her. Just before he left, he saw the worst of her, yet when his anger cooled, there was still love.

The words might have been true twelve years ago, but now Justin had seen the real worst of her. The letter crinkled and crackled as she shoved it back into the envelope. No love could overcome what she'd done.

Coffee this morning was not hitting its mark. Taryn's second official day of Christmas break. It would be better if there were school to go to. She wouldn't have to think about anything from yesterday. She'd have more to do than stand in front of the fireplace in her pj's and catalog the pathetic number of presents under her tree. Most of them were for Jemma.

Well, not exactly. In a normal year, most of them would be for Jemma. This year, there were more Ethan toys than Jemma gifts.

Her lips curved around the rim of her coffee mug. It had been fun back in July when she'd impulsively started buying presents. Good thing since she certainly was not in the mood now. She toed a wrapped package farther under the tree. Maybe someone would cancel Christmas this year. Or postpone it until next year.

Her great-grandmother's grandfather clock gonged seven times. It might still be too early to go to Jemma's. Yeah, her grandmother typically got up as soon as the sun peeked over the edge of the world, but after the stress of the past week, today might be an exception

Eight. At eight Taryn would head over to the house and tell her grandmother she was sorry for racing out like she did. Jemma may have told her to leave, but she still shouldn't have gone.

Draining her coffee down to the bottom of the cup, Taryn walked across the room and twisted the blinds open just as Marnie's little pickup eased into the short driveway. There was only one reason she'd be there this early in the morning. Jemma must have sent her.

Taryn set her coffee cup on the end table and yanked open the front door. "Jemma made you come over?"

"Shh." Marnie laid a finger on her lips, slipped out of the truck holding a Styrofoam coffee cup in each hand, and eased the door closed with her elbows. "You're going to wake the neighbors." She took the first step and held out a cup.

"I have coffee."

"I see, but this is a mocha with a double shot. I had a feeling you'd need a little extra get up and go this morning, so I drove all the way to Dalton for it. You're going to drink it." Marnie pressed the cup into Taryn's hand and squeezed by her into the living room, plopping herself into the recliner near the fireplace. "So . . . ?" She arched her eyebrow like a question mark over her own coffee.

Taryn sank onto the hearth beside the chair and took a cautious sip. Perfect. "I guess you being here and peddling caffeine to me answers my first question, huh?"

"Yes, Jemma sent me to talk to you."

"How much did she tell you?" While Taryn had run to Marnie often, she'd hidden Sarah's existence deep, even from her grandmother's best friend. She'd felt too ashamed, had feared too much what Marnie would think if she ever found out what Taryn did.

Marnie laid a hand on the top of Taryn's head, letting it rest there until the warmth seeped from her fingers into Taryn's heart. "Nothing. Mostly she wanted me to check on you."

"So she didn't tell you she up and said Justin almost proposed to me a million years ago?" The coffee cup hit against the brick hearth.

"What?" Marnie pulled her hand back so fast Taryn reached for her coffee to keep it from slinging across the room. "When?"

It still hurt to say it out loud. "Like I said, a million years ago."

Marnie set her eye on Taryn and refused to look away.

"C'mon, Marn." Taryn was weary with the weight of everything. "You brought me mocha. With a double shot. You're supposed to be cheering me up, right? Wasn't your mission to be a ray of sunshine?"

"We need to talk." The way Marnie held her gaze was too penetrating.

Taryn looked down at the cup in her hands.

"Look," Marnie finally sighed, turning the cup from side to side in her palm. "I know."

"Because I just told you. I guess he was going to—"

"No." She set the cup on the floor and angled toward Taryn. "I know everything."

"Everything?" Taryn's voice was as thin and weak as the mews of the kittens they once found out in the barn, holed up in a stack of old apple baskets. "Even . . ."

"Everything."

Taryn slid off the short hearth to the floor beside Marnie, wrapped her arms around her legs, and leaned against Marnie, looking for a strong place to land. "Jemma told you?"

Marnie's laugh was soft and sympathetic. "I've known you your whole life. In fact, I'd venture to guess the only person who knows you better than your grandmother does is me. I knew when you left for college something was up. Then when you didn't come home for Christmas . . . You turned into a moping recluse. When you transferred back here to come to school, it didn't take much to put it all together."

"You never said anything."

"I went to Jemma and asked her. She might be a lot of things, but she's never been a good liar."

Taryn's eyes rolled up to the ceiling, and she pulled her knees tighter to her chest. "Yes, she has. Just not to you."

"Honey, she did what she thought was best."

"Doesn't make it right."

"No, it doesn't. And I'm not going to condone it." Cool fingers rested on Taryn's neck, stealing some of the heat from her frustration. "But put yourself in her shoes. Your dad was horrible to your mom, to you . . . the two most important people in her life."

"Justin wouldn't be like that."

"You know he wouldn't now because you see him all grown up. But, Taryn, your grandmother had no way of knowing, and she was too scared to take the chance. You know how she's talked about your dad. They treated him like a son. Your grandpa went hunting and fishing with him. He was good people. Then you came along. Maybe your mom did it on purpose to keep him here and maybe she didn't, but he resented you from the moment he heard about you. It used to break my heart, watching you as a little girl, looking for his approval. I think he's the reason why you and I got so close because the mama-hurt in me just wanted to make up for what he wasn't giving." She let her hand drop to Taryn's back and rubbed a small circle there. "What you don't know is, when your father turned ugly, your mama was planning to walk away and raise you on her own. Jemma talked your mother into marrying him, into doing the right thing. She thought things would change, and once you were born your daddy wouldn't be able to resist you. He'd see giving up a job wasn't worth giving up a family."

"She was wrong." This was the worst part, the hardest pill of all to swallow. Jemma had never been wrong. All of Taryn's life, she'd been the dispenser of wise advice, the one who always knew just what to say to make it all work out. Now she'd been wrong. Hugely, tragically, horribly wrong twice, in life-altering, unchangeable ways.

"It's why she went the opposite way with you and Justin."

"It didn't work." Taryn shoved off the hearth and fingered the ornaments on her tiny Christmas tree, the one she'd decorated with Justin only a few days ago. Her mom's baby handprint forever molded in clay dangled from a branch just above her own tiny handprint, an empty space beneath. Justin had tried to hang a red ball there, but she'd moved it. The space was empty. Always.

"She was trying to help. Taryn, honey, she didn't want to see you suffer."

The empty branch whipped back and forth as Taryn flicked it. "But I did. I do. Maybe I was just being selfish, and she convinced me it was the best thing for me, not necessarily for the baby. Everything turned out okay for Sarah, but what if it hadn't?"

"I kind of thought you might be thinking about every-thing this morning." Marnie appeared beside her. "Think about your cousin and Ethan." She sniffed, looked at the ceiling, smiled. "Crazy timing if I ever saw it. Mark and Rachel are more ready to start a family than anyone I've ever seen. It was a blow to her when she found out she might not be able to have kids, but before she could even grieve . . ." Marnie shrugged and grinned. "Along comes Ethan, before they can even get the house finished and get married. Perfect and wonderful and an answer to prayer, just not quite when they were expecting the answer. They could have told Ethan's birth mother no, the timing was wrong, but it would have been sort of telling God they knew better, don't you think? God took care of Sarah. Let go of this guilt, and let Him take care of you now."

Taryn brushed away the last of Marnie's sentence. "Ethan's different. His mother was totally unable to take care of him."

"Could you have raised a baby? At eighteen? With a high school education and no job and totally incapable of accept-ing or giving the kind of unconditional love your daughter needed?"

"What?"

"Listen." Marnie pushed herself out of the recliner and reached for Taryn, pulling her close in a soft embrace. "You were just about as broken as any human being I've seen. People as hurt as you go looking for something to fill the spot, only instead of turning to drugs or alcohol or work, you turned to people. Justin was your addiction, and you were always afraid he'd vanish."

"He did vanish. And I wasn't addicted to him." The words muffled into Marnie's shoulder.

"You were, and you shoved him away. Your dad had your head screwed on so backward, you wouldn't know love if it slapped you sideways."

She was so wrong. "I loved Justin."

"Think about what you're saying. Did you ever truly believe he loved you back, so much he'd give almost anything for you?"

"He didn't stay."

"You never should have asked him to." Marnie huffed her exasperation and set Taryn away, planting warm hands on her shoulders and forcing Taryn to look at her. "And you never believed he truly loved you. You forget I was there. You came over to my house quite often and talked to me. There was always your fear inside, certain he'd find someone prettier, smarter, better. You gave and gave and gave, trying to keep him until you snapped inside and couldn't give anymore. It wasn't love. Not the kind God intended. It was this desperate closed-handed love, like you kept thinking you had to earn it, as if you could will it into existence and into lasting."

The words Taryn had said to Chelsea chased Marnie's in a circle. *Love isn't something you earn. It's not something you have to be good enough for. Real love is freely given, not taken away because you trip and fall.*

The mirror Taryn had always looked into cracked. Marnie was right. *She* was right. And she'd always known better. "No matter what I did, I was never good enough for my dad to love me."

"So you assumed the same of everyone. Even God." Marnie angled around to get directly into Taryn's field of vision. "God is not going to punish you for giving up your baby. He's not going to make Jemma die because you did some horrifically wrong thing. Stop expecting Him to."

The tears pricked behind Taryn's eyes, dug into her throat, pushed themselves out to leak down her cheek. "You think I've been expecting God to punish me?" But she didn't have to ask. It was true. She'd lied. She'd made excuses for the lies, believing them herself. And all those years, she'd waited for punishment. Discipline came in the form of her lie's consequences, not in the form of a God waiting to fling flaming arrows at her.

Marnie pulled her close. "Go to Jemma. Tell her you forgive her."

Taryn nodded. There was a lot needing to be said there. And most of it should have been said years ago.

Backing away, Marnie pressed her palms to Taryn's cheeks. "Go to Justin. Tell him you're sorry."

Asking for forgiveness would be beyond impossible. "It's a huge thing to ask."

Marnie smiled slightly and shook her head. "Taryn, my love, you might be surprised."

16

What are you doing New Year's . . . New Year's Eve? Harry Connick Jr. crooned to Taryn through Jemma's back door.

Well, Harry, I'm going to a wedding in a couple of weeks. The one that started this whole mess because the stinking quilt had to be ready just in time. Thanks for asking. Oh, and I'll be going alone too. Just in case your happily married self was thinking I might need a plus one.

Laying one hand against the wood frame of the old white screen door, Taryn gripped the handle and felt for the first time that she should knock before entering her own grandmother's house, the house she'd practically grown up in. She'd fallen so far in the past twenty-four hours.

Only twenty-four hours. Even less, since they stepped in the house and everything changed. Taryn had spent the night staring at her ceiling, praying, wanting to call Jemma or come over but wanting to know the forgiveness bubbling in her wasn't just going to be words. It had to be real. If she lost Jemma, she lost everything, but the last thing either of them needed was for Taryn to forgive her for the wrong reasons or in a half-hearted, incomplete way.

It had taken Marnie's wisdom to show her what forgiveness was. Now, after some serious God time, Taryn made the choice to forgive Jemma. Maybe someday, Justin would forgive her, even if he never loved her again.

All prepared to let out a world-weary sigh, Taryn inhaled and stopped. It smelled like . . .

It was. Cake. Jemma was making cake.

One-handed.

At nine o'clock in the morning.

The door handle twisted in Taryn's hands, responding to the siren's call of warm cake and the coffee bound to be waiting in the carafe on the counter.

"You going to stand out there all day, or are you coming in?" Jemma's face appeared in the curtains by the door. "It's colder than the inside of the Grinch's tiny little heart out there." She disappeared, then the door popped open and there she was, eye-to-eye with Taryn one step down from her, the only thing between them the flimsy screen and every past secret that came to light yesterday. The events of the past day lay heavy on Jemma's face, her eyes scanning Taryn's warily.

Face-to-face with her grandmother, all of Taryn's planned apologies died before they even hit her tongue. "You made cake."

"Of course I did."

"You only have one working arm right now."

"And I have a nice stand mixer to hold the batter bowl for me. I'm behind on baking. Seriously behind. Got cookies in the oven. And a caramel cake on the counter. But you know . . . the cake. I couldn't get the icing the way it needs to be, so somebody's just going to have to eat it."

Taryn sniffed, tears pricking the back of her eyes. Jemma worked when she was upset. And she made caramel cake as a big ol' giant *I love you.* "Only if there's coffee, Old Woman."

Jemma smiled at the familiar nickname, used so often in gentle rebuke. She knew she was doing so much more than the doctor had given her permission to do and, likely, she didn't care. "There's always coffee."

The words were barely cleared out of the air before somehow, the door was open and Taryn was pressed tight in the kind of hug only her grandmother could give. "I'm so sorry, baby girl. I wanted to tell you about the letter, but it just got harder and harder. And I always knew the longer I waited, the angrier you'd be. You don't know how many nights Justin's letter kept me awake, how many prayers have been said over it."

Taryn took her first deep breath since the day before and relaxed into her grandmother's one–armed hug. There was no anger left. Just relief. Jemma still loved her. "It's me who's sorry." Taryn kissed the top of her hair.

"For what?" Jemma edged her back, holding Taryn's upper arm with her one useful hand. Her forehead wrinkled. "What do you have to be sorry for?"

"Leaving you here yesterday the way I did." Guilt was the other thing keeping her up all night. "I was angry."

"And you should have been." She squeezed Taryn's bicep tighter. "I told you to leave. You needed time to yourself to think through everything. You have to stop apologizing when you haven't done anything wrong. Save your sorrys for when you need them."

"But—"

"You had every right to be angry. Every right. I was wrong. I lied to you. I hurt you. For you to bust out of here would have been justified, and I'm downright surprised with your McKenna temper, you didn't take my screen door off the hinges on the way out. Think about it. What would have happened if you'd stayed?"

All of the ugly words bouncing around in her head as she'd sped home yesterday scrolled back through, but Jemma didn't need to hear them then or now. Taryn shrugged.

Chuckling, Jemma patted her arm. "Taryn, you are cut from the same cloth as your grandmother. I know the things you were thinking ought to have you facedown at the altar on Sunday morning."

Finally, Jemma managed to drag a smile to Taryn's face.

"Besides, Marnie was here and was just what the doctor ordered. She follows me when I get spun up and need to work it through." Jemma reached for Taryn's hand and pulled her into the house. "Come here. You need to see this."

Following Jemma through the house, Taryn's head turned as they passed the kitchen where the buttery rich smell of fresh caramel icing tugged almost harder than Jemma. Cookies cooled on racks all over the counter, and several tins were filled and stacked by the sink. "How long have you been up?"

"Watched the sun rise this morning. It was beautiful. You know, I couldn't see either sunrise or sunset out my blamed hospital window? I missed it."

The guilt stabbed Taryn again. Jemma should be resting. Her heart—

"And don't you apologize again either. I know you're thinking it. My heart is just fine, and trust me, I got plenty of rest in the hospital. My medicine's all fixed, and my heart's happy to be home. With my granddaughter." She squeezed

Taryn's hand and pulled her into the den, stopping and stepping aside for Taryn to step around her.

It looked like a fabric triage. The two old plastic card tables from the barn dominated the room, topped with Jemma's good sewing machine and her smaller travel model. Blue-and-white fabric spilled out of plastic shoeboxes, and strips lay folded neatly along the back of the couch.

Taryn's heart beat faster. "What is this?"

"I told you. Marnie followed me while I worked things through. We sewed until almost one in the morning."

"You can't deal with your emotions, so you work."

"My fingers to the bone." Jemma smiled softly and gave Taryn a light hug. "I had to sort through the relief of you knowing the truth and the pain you were feeling. Marnie helped. She listened. And she sewed through the yawns to keep me company."

"Another quilt?" Again with the quilts? Taryn didn't care at this point if she never saw another one. Nor did she care what Jemma had done with the one Justin and she had sewn. For all Taryn cared, it had been thrown in the cheerily popping fireplace the moment her foot hit the bottom step on her way out yesterday.

The thought sent a pang against her heart. Not really, but denying the truth about her emotions made her feel a little bit better.

Pride and excitement warred for prominence in Jemma's expression. "Rachel's wedding is a little over a week away. With some help, we can get her a proper quilt done in time. And Holly can put a rush on quilting it as long as I get it to her four days ahead of time. I already spoke to her."

"When?"

"Yesterday evening."

Of course. When did Jemma ever wait on anyone? She probably called smack in the middle of dinner, while Holly was eating, then charmed her until the woman thought the idea of a rush quilting was her own.

"It's not hand-sewn." Wasn't Jemma's biggest thing the method of construction? An heirloom quilt must be sewn by hand, or it was not an heirloom.

"Yes, well, Marnie and I were talking." Of course they were. "And it's more important for Rachel to have a quilt than it is for it be hand-sewn. The look on her face . . . Won't it be worth the work?"

Still. Taryn's fingers and her heart both ached from the hours with Justin. And speaking of hearts . . . "You know the doctor told you to be careful with—"

"My heart is happy. And it will be happier when Rachel opens up her own Irish chain. It'll be like her mama was here. Tying her together in her family's history is what she needs. Working toward it for her is what I need." Tears hung on the edges of her lashes. "Rachel's new family is the most important thing." Jemma swiped at her eyes, cheeks pinking with embarrassment over her rare show of emotion, and slapped her hands together. "Now, there is cake to eat. Wait." She turned on Taryn. "Did you have breakfast?"

Taryn shook her head.

"Then you definitely need cake. And afterward, we'll box up cookies, and you can help me sew." Jemma was off again, huffing to the kitchen and muttering about fresh coffee.

Taryn let a smile tip the corner of her mouth. Jemma. Nothing slowed her down. Not a heart condition. Not a broken arm. And not the sadness for Taryn and Justin lurking behind her eyes.

—∞∞∞—

When the pounding on her front door came after midnight, Taryn didn't have to guess who it was. Justin was not about phone calls. It only made sense he'd show up in person to ask the questions only she could answer.

She sat up in the bed, letting the covers pool around her waist, and pulled on the App State sweatshirt she'd discarded on the pillow beside her only an hour ago. The pounding continued as she pulled on thick socks and padded to the door, knowing she should hurry, but scared into slow motion by what was sure to be righteous anger.

The front door squeaked its protest at the late hour as Taryn pulled it open. "Justin." She didn't even pretend he'd interrupted her sleep.

He stepped away until he stood about six feet from the door, near her porch swing, wearing jeans and his ever-present jacket, twisting her heart with the familiarity of the sight. He kept his back to her, staring across the side yard toward the Jenkins house next door. "Tell me about the baby."

Small talk wasn't something she'd expected, but neither was this kind of abruptness. In her mind, Taryn had pictured him angry and loud and ranting, not quiet and to the point. Then again, this was Justin, and she'd only seen him angry once. At her. This quiet was almost scarier, but she deserved it. With a sigh, she tested the door to make sure it was unlocked, then pulled it closed behind her. When the screen door slipped shut, she sank into the white porch rocker. Her legs wouldn't hold her, she was sure. "What do you want to know?"

"Everything." Even the day they'd parted on his parents' front lawn, Justin had never sounded like this. It was like he strained for the words. He was not only angry, he was hurt, just like Taryn had known he'd be. But knowing it and confronting it in person were two different things.

She'd caused it—the pain in his voice. Taryn pulled her knees to her chest and wrapped her arms around her flannel-clad shins. "I'm sorry." The words weren't big enough. Nothing would ever be big enough. It made her stomach ache.

Keeping his back to her, Justin tilted his head toward the ceiling. "I can't do an apology right now. I'm not there yet. Just tell me about him or her. Was it a boy or a girl?"

If he ever got to where he could hear her apologize, it would be a miracle. At this point, it would take a miracle to even get him to look in her direction again. "There's no *was*. She didn't *die*. She was *adopted*. She's a girl. Sarah."

"Sarah." He seemed to try the name on for size. "Sarah what?" There was a touch of wonder tingeing the heaviness.

"Sarah Faith. Because her parents had prayed so long . . ." Taryn had forgotten the conversation until now. It solidified the answer to her earlier question and proved Marnie's words. The Warrens had waited so long for a child, and Sarah had been the answer to their prayers. "I was going to church in Pennsylvania, and I met the Warrens. They'd been praying for a child, and then I showed up and—"

"So you know who adopted her? You've seen her? Had contact with her?"

"Only in pictures. I have her school pictures. They're inside. Her parents write a few times a year. I send a present on her birthday and Christmas. I haven't ever seen her in person. Not even on the day she was born." Her gut twisted again in a way all too familiar. It wouldn't have been fair to Sarah or to Justin to physically be with the little girl, and Sarah had never asked, until now. Something told her this was not the time to bring up Sarah's most recent letter.

There was a silence so long Taryn thought he might have no more questions, but then he breathed in his measured way, the one where he was furious and was doing his best to hold his temper.

It was cold out here, but his silence made the air feel ten degrees colder, like a sudden front had swept off the mountain. It ran along her skin under her sweatshirt and raised goose bumps along her arms.

"Do you realize what you took from me when you gave her away without ever letting me know she existed?" Justin spoke like he'd been holding the words back for a long time and, once he started talking, they wouldn't be stopped. He gripped the porch rail beside him. "You gave our child . . . Did you hear me, Taryn? *Our* child away, and you never even asked me. You never even took what I'd think or what I'd feel into consideration. Life could be so much different right now if you'd told me."

"You're right." When his anger burst, so did hers. All of the grief she'd held back for so long tumbled out in a furious rush. "Life would have been different. Because you'd have married me. You'd have done the right thing, and before she was even born, you'd have hated me and resented her. We were eighteen, Justin. Eighteen. Neither of us was ready. It would have been horrible."

Silence again. The grandfather clock in the living room chimed a muffled half hour before he spoke again, low and measured. "Is that what you think of me?"

"This is not about you right now. This is about the you who was already feeling like I'd used you. This is about the kids we were. Some part of you would have always believed I got pregnant on purpose to trap you. I did the right thing for all three of us. In the wrong way, yes, but don't you ever, ever act like it was easy for me." Taryn swallowed the sting of tears trying to rush from her stomach and out her eyeballs. "It wasn't. It has never been easy. Not for one day."

"Seems to me like you don't have any right to be angry here." Justin's voice rose. "You're not the one who was lied to, who was treated like he didn't even exist in his own daughter's life. You're not the one who has missed every single birthday and every single Christmas. She's what? Twelve now?"

"Eleven."

"And she's called someone else dad all of this time." The bitter anger coming across the porch was so much worse than the hurt from earlier.

"The Warrens love her a lot, Justin." For the first time, it occurred to her Justin could challenge the adoption as Sarah's birth father, even all these years later. Taryn sat straighter, her feet thudding to the wood porch, panic hammering her pulse so hard she could feel it in her head. "Justin. Don't try to take her away from them. They've been the best thing for her."

"Once again, this is how little you think of me." He huffed, breath visible in the chilled air. "I would never . . . but it doesn't mean I condone what you did. You lied. You had to lie to have her . . . Sarah . . . given away without my consent."

"I did." Admitting it out loud hurt worse than almost anything else. It brought to the surface all of the guilt she'd managed to absorb, destroyed all of the excuses she'd managed to make. God may have forgiven her, but the guilt stuck firm.

"What did you tell them?"

This was the hardest part. "I didn't know who the father was."

More silence. "You erased me and made yourself out to be . . . to be that?" His laugh was bitter. "So let me ask you this. You're sure I'm her father?"

Taryn winced at the angry accusation, but she deserved it. "Positive. There was only you. One time."

"Only me." Justin practically whispered it, turning his eyes skyward. "I knew after twelve years you'd be different and I'd be different. Still, all the time we spent together, made me think . . . it was stupid."

"What was stupid?" Taryn was terrified to ask, but she had to know what he was hinting.

"I was stupid." A car passed on School Street, and he waited for it to disappear around the curve toward town. "Forget it. Is there anything else you're not telling me?"

The letter. Sarah's request. What would it do to the girl to find out Taryn had known who her real father was all along? Would it thrill her or make her just as angry at Taryn as Justin was? If it made the girl angry, if it made the Warrens angry, Taryn deserved it. She'd caused the problem; she'd have to face the consequences.

"Taryn, what are you not telling me? This is one time you'd better not hold one thing back."

She swallowed hard and pulled in a deep breath, the cold stinging her lungs. "I got a letter this week." The words hung up in her throat. It was better if he saw for himself. "Know what? I'll get the letters and you can read them all."

Taryn pulled the door open and slipped her hand in, pulling the letters from the table by the door. She'd laid them there last night, knowing he'd eventually show up looking for answers.

Justin was waiting at the foot of the steps, and he kept his fingers far from hers as he took the stack. "I'll get these back to you. Eventually." He walked across the yard, shoulders hunched against the cold and with the weight of Taryn's burden.

His truck rumbled to life and he was gone, having never looked at Taryn once.

17

Every eye in the church was on Taryn.

At least, it felt like it. The truth was out there. Marnie knew. Justin knew. There was no telling who else did too.

It had been four days since he'd walked away from her carrying those letters. It was his story to tell, and he could tell whoever he wanted. Right then, it felt like he'd told everybody, and every whisper rippling across the sanctuary and rising up to the wood beams in the ceiling felt like it was saying her name. It would be a miracle if she got through the Christmas Eve service without losing her head in a panic attack and screaming the truth to everyone in the pews of Hollings Christian.

If fear won, she'd miss her favorite part of Christmas. After the congregation sang "Joy to the World," when the church went dark and the gathered voices joined for "Silent Night," everyone lit individual candles and filed quietly out into the dark before heading home to await Christmas morning. It always filled Taryn's heart with Jesus, with the fact He had come.

And she was forgiven.

Rachel slid in beside Taryn and plopped Ethan into her lap. Taryn jumped and grabbed for the small boy before he could slide onto the floor. "Well, hello there." Just what God ordered. Distraction in the form of cuteness.

Ethan grinned his sloppy grin and patted a fat palm against her cheek.

Taryn grinned back and trapped his fingers between her lips, shaking her head slightly just to hear his rolling baby giggle.

"You looked like you could use a smile, and Ethan's the perfect weapon. Where's Jemma?" Rachel pulled off her gloves and stuffed them in her coat pocket, glancing around.

"Taking in a hem in one of the shepherd's robes. Isaiah Reynolds keeps tripping. She's going to stay back there and help them change. She said she can hear enough from the back." Hopefully. According to the bulletin, the choir was singing her favorite, "O Holy Night."

Rachel held her hands out for Ethan, but like he knew Taryn needed the comfort, he snuggled up to her, tucking his head under her chin and stuffing his thumb in his mouth like he was settling in for the long haul.

"Guess he's happy there." Rachel shrugged and let her gaze wander the room.

"Where's Mark?"

"Hm?" Rachel glanced at her and went back to rubbernecking. She was as nosy as Mrs. Jenkins, always wanting to know who was where and who was with whom. "Mark's on duty tonight at the station in Dalton. He'll be off for Christmas tomorrow. He's going to come over in the morning and pick Ethan and me up and take us over to the house." She grinned. "He put up a tree in our big ol' empty living room and is bound and determined Ethan will have his first Christmas morning with us there as a family, even if there isn't any furniture there and we aren't officially a family yet."

Taryn's heart twisted. "How beautiful. Mark's a good man."

"'Bout time I hung onto him, huh?" Rachel frowned. "I wasted too many years running away. But he never gave up."

"Good thing." Taryn swallowed the tang of jealousy and nuzzled the top of Ethan's precious head, inhaling tear-free shampoo and the plain ol' scent of little boy. Her eyes drifted shut, and it was an effort to push away the pain of never having known the feeling. Of never having even held her own baby.

She forced her eyes open. Her baby, who was better off where she was, with loving parents prepared for a baby when the time came. Parents who chose her baby to love. Their baby to love. Look at Ethan. Rachel and Mark could not be better parents, all because someone made the hard choice.

With the letter from Sarah last week, Taryn no longer had to know the void of not looking her in the eye. More than anything, she wanted to go to Sarah and build whatever relationship God wanted them to have.

Peace settled over her soul as the children's choir filed in. At least for Sarah, Taryn knew she'd done the right thing, and the knowledge was more important than any grief.

Still, it was almost more than she could bear watching the kids do their pageant. The three wise men were particularly hard to watch, the older kids full of their importance, eleven years old, just the right age. Taryn squeezed Ethan again, and he squawked, then reached for his mama.

Taryn hefted him over with a smacky kiss on his forehead and settled back in to watch the miracle of baby Jesus coming to earth to save.

The children spoke their lines, the parents sighed, and the shepherds knelt, then the lights in the small sanctuary came up, blinding against the white walls. Children made awkward bows and filed down the center aisle to change back into their clothes and find their parents as the preacher stepped up to the stage.

Ray Phipps had been the preacher at Hollings Christian for as long as Taryn could remember. Tonight, his grandson was in the play for the first time, a tiny shepherd with a crook almost too big for him. Anyone could see the pride all over Ray's face as he watched the kids walk out. "Aren't our kids something?"

More smattering applause and a few whoops from proud daddies.

Ray grinned, then grew slightly more serious. But only slightly. "Before we sing a couple of songs and light the candles as is our tradition, I just want to say something."

Funny. He usually started the singing, letting the kids do all of the showing.

"Somebody needs to hear this tonight." Ray stepped off the platform and stood right in front of the altar. "Love came down at Christmas. You all already know the story." He walked over to Taryn's side of the church and scanned the crowd. "Not because we asked for it. Not because we deserved it. But because it's how God is. Unconditional. No matter what we do." With a nod, as though he'd done his duty, he stepped back up on the platform and called for the congregation to open their hymnals to "Joy to the World."

Taryn's fingers fumbled. *Somebody needs to hear this tonight.* It was her. It had to be. It was almost the exact same thing Marnie had said last week. The exact same words had echoed in her head ever since. *So what are you saying exactly, God?*

The voice of the crowd swelled around her, but Taryn still heard it. Almost a whisper. *I love you. No matter what. I always have.* Peace washed over her like never before. She closed her eyes and dropped her head, refusing to cry even here, even now, because there were too many people. But still . . . all along, ever since Justin and Taryn did what they did, she'd felt God's disapproval. She'd heard her father's voice every time she prayed. *Nuisance. Annoyance.* But God had never felt those things. He'd been waiting all along with open arms, waiting for her to hear, and he'd sent Marnie, the preacher, her own heart to tell her. It was the love she'd been missing, the love she hadn't been prepared to give to her child or to Justin because she wasn't ready to accept it from God. Her arms erupted in warm chills sending a shudder through her. *You are loved. No matter what.*

She was sinking into the peaceful feeling when Rachel elbowed her in the ribs. "I thought Justin and his dad went to church in Dalton."

Leave me alone. God and I are having a moment.

She elbowed again. "Taryn."

"Yes." She hissed. "As far as I know." *Now leave me and God alone.*

"So why is he here?"

Taryn jerked her head up and followed Rachel's gaze across the room. Near the front on the left were shoulders she recognized without fail, next to his father, whose hymnal trembled slightly as he sang.

Her fingers gripped the hymnal tighter, watching, unable to look away from his unexpected appearance and definitely not wanting to look at Rachel. She'd start asking questions.

As if he could feel her gaze, Justin glanced over his shoulder, and his eyes found Taryn's, empty and dark. She wanted to look away. She wanted to mouth *I'm sorry*. She wanted to turn back time. But before anything could happen, the lights cut and he was too far away to see.

Before the first candle could be lit, Taryn pushed past Rachel and out into the aisle, bolting for freedom, for home, where she wouldn't have to face him.

18

Simply Having a Wonderful Christmastime" blared out of the alarm clock at six on Christmas morning. Taryn slapped her hand down on the snooze and buried her head under the pillow, muttering, "Shut up, Paul McCartney." It was too early in the morning after a night with not nearly enough sleep. After several nights with not nearly enough sleep if the honesty train was chugging through town.

She missed Justin. There. She'd thought it in words and not just in vague, aching emotions. Somewhere in the deepest part of her, there had been the barely formed idea they'd at least see each other on Christmas this year, and the whole new year would be a whole new beginning for them, where somehow she'd find a way to tell him the truth on her terms, and he'd be okay with it.

Kind of like Harry's "Christmas Dreaming" crooning over at Jemma's last night during dinner. Dreaming got you nowhere, Harry, but the thought was nice.

Taryn rolled over and pulled the sheets tighter around her, Justin's letter crinkling as her arm made contact. No matter how many times she'd read it last night, she couldn't wrap her head around it and make it real. The what ifs just wouldn't leave her alone when her eyes closed.

The covers slid down to her waist as she sat up in bed and switched off the alarm for real, then dragged her hands back through her hair. Lying in bed wouldn't do anybody any good. No matter what her life looked like, she couldn't deny what day it was. God was good, and Christmas proved it.

Besides, Jemma was waiting for her to come and have their traditional Christmas breakfast.

What was there to mope about anyway? Jemma admired her own Christmas tree at home instead of lying in the hospital with a tiny Charlie Brown tree for company. Her recovery made this better than every other Christmas.

With a crackle of protest, Justin's letter went into the top drawer of her nightstand. Taryn slipped her Bible over and flipped to Matthew for a healthy dose of what this day was about. It for sure wasn't all about her.

Or was it? Her finger tapped verse twenty-three, highlighted in neon orange at some point long ago. *Immanuel. God with us.* With her. God gave up His child to do what was best for His children. For her. Because He loved her. Even when she'd royally, royally messed up.

Lord, I did all of the right things for all of the wrong reasons. Except lying. Lying was the wrong thing no matter what the reason. It was time she let go of it all, from her dad up to the lie she'd told Justin by never telling him anything at all.

This new beginning would start with a face-to-face apology. Chances were high he'd never look her in the eye, but he deserved the whole truth, even if he hated her.

With a new peace and a new resolve, Taryn set her Bible aside and headed for the kitchen for coffee, stopping by her tree to lay a finger on her mother's tiny handprint, then on her own, then in the space beneath, finally at peace with Sarah's life.

Her fingers trailed across the branches to the miniature Fred ornament Justin had found somewhere and slipped onto her tree. *I could have fallen in love with you for real this time.*

She had. Taryn cupped the little truck in her hand and let its weight rest, not surprised by the revelation. She'd known it from the moment he sat beside her in the hospital waiting room, and he'd only confirmed it by stitching on the quilt with her, hauling Jemma a tree, bringing movies to the hospital . . .

Marnie said real love didn't have conditions. Something told Taryn that Justin had already figured love out. A flick to the truck set it swinging slightly. A good truck and a good man. She'd shoved them both away.

But this day was about Jesus and her so, walking into the kitchen on the trail of fresh-brewed coffee, Taryn thanked God for her auto-start coffeemaker. It was definitely one of His good gifts.

Her favorite thick white mug full of coffee sent warmth up her arms and into her soul. And maybe . . . "C'mon, God. Can we have a white Christmas this year?" The drizzly snow of the past few weeks gave her hope, but to be honest, Hollings wasn't known for snow this time of year.

Using the coffee cup, Taryn eased back the curtain over her sink and peeked at the backyard. Nothing but muddy dead grass.

Back through the kitchen and into the den. Like a kid checking for a snow day, something in her hoped maybe there'd been a blizzard in the front yard and it had simply missed the back.

One peek through the blinds dashed her hope. She backed away and started to drop the blinds, but the sun peeked over the edge of the world and highlighted a hulking shape in her front yard.

What is . . . ?

There was a truck in her driveway. For one brief instant, her heart skipped. Justin. But it wasn't. The cab was too small. In fact, it was a single cab. Like . . .

"Fred."

Her hands gripped the coffee mug tighter as the day grew gradually lighter. It couldn't be Fred. He was so long gone, he must be in the junkyard in Craymont by now, or on somebody's back forty rusting.

A Christmas wish she hadn't even known she wanted, spoken out loud on a whim to Justin, the only one who knew.

Setting the coffee mug on the window ledge, Taryn raced through the kitchen to find her boots by the door, dragged them on, and hit the driveway in a splash of mud that coated the bottoms of her pajamas.

Circling the truck, she studied it from all angles. It was Fred, down to the dent in the rear bumper where she'd backed into one of Jemma's pecan trees when Grampa was teaching her how to drive. Jemma didn't make her caramel cake for months.

It was Fred, but not like the last time she'd seen him. He was polished in all of his blue-and-white glory for Christmas.

Justin was the only one who knew she missed Fred, unless he'd told Jemma. He must have told her because there was no way he'd do something like this. It was too extravagant. Too much like love.

She reached out a hand and let it hover near the door. If she touched him, would he vanish? Taking the chance, she closed her eyes and gripped the door handle, then peeked. Fred was still there. A grin split her face clean in two.

Dropping her head against the side window, she ran her hand down the door between the window and the frame and whispered, "I'm sorry I sold you off."

"It's a truck, not a horse, you know."

Her fingers tightened on the door handle. Fred might be real and in her driveway, but the voice had to be a hallucination.

"I'm pretty sure he doesn't have feelings." The voice again. "Then again, it's Fred, so he might. I'd imagine you owe him that apology, selling him the way you did."

Taryn let go of the door handle and turned slowly. If she moved too fast, she might wake up.

Justin sat on her white porch swing, blue-jeaned legs stretched out and crossed at the ankles, hands stuffed in the pockets of his work coat.

Chills pricked Taryn's arms and worked their way down her legs. Suddenly, she was aware of her blue flannel pj pants, sweatshirt, and hiking boots. Her hands flew to her head. No telling what her hair looked like.

"You look fine, McKenna." His voice grew huskier.

"I look like I just woke up." The words squeaked out.

He shrugged. "You look about right for Christmas morning."

"What are you doing here?" She wished the words sounded more polite because she wanted him there, even if her question didn't quite telegraph it.

He stood, walked to the rail, and braced his hands, never looking away from her. "I had to bring Fred."

"Why?"

"Christmas Day, Christmas present . . . makes sense."

Taryn sank against Fred, knees refusing to hold her anymore. A tiny flicker of hope lit behind her heart. "Justin, I—"

He held up a hand. "I've been doing a lot of thinking. You know, if you treat trucks right they'll be there forever. They'll give you everything they've got, but you have to put love into them." He drew his arms in and gripped the rail tighter, looking at Fred. "But you beat a truck up, don't give it what it needs, it'll quit on you. It can't lay out what it doesn't take in."

"You came over here to give me a lesson in mechanics?"

"No. I came to bring Fred home." Justin threw his arms wide. "Merry Christmas."

Taryn felt behind her for the door, looking for something solid in this down-the-rabbit-hole morning. "You did this?"

"I did."

"Why? After what I did . . ."

"Because you wanted Fred. And I wanted you to have everything you wanted."

"But—"

"And I wanted to hear what you had to say. The whole story. About us." The slight cockiness he wore cracked. "About Sarah."

Her early morning prayer floated through Taryn's mind. *Apologize. While you have the chance.* She wanted to push away from the truck and swish through the muddy grass to him, but her legs would never make it. The chills had led to trembling, whether from the cold or the confrontation, she wasn't sure.

From this angle, he was looking down at her. It was fitting. She didn't deserve eye level. "I'm sorry." Her voice cracked around words too long in coming. "I should've told you." All she had left was a whisper.

"Yeah, you should've. What you did was rotten and . . . wrong."

She could only nod, not trusting her words.

"How do you feel about it all now?" Justin looked like a lot hinged on the question.

The building peace burst forth. "Sarah's had a better life than we could have given her. I couldn't have been a good mom. I was too messed up." He had to understand, even if he couldn't forgive her.

"I was angry after I found out. Angrier than I've ever been at anyone and, believe me, the army can make you pretty angry. But God has this crazy way . . ." Justin shoved his hands in his pockets. "I'd picked up Fred from Bob two days before Jemma aired everything. Wouldn't you know, the only place to channel my energy was your confounded truck. First, I figured I'd sell it, maybe try to let you feel how much you hurt me."

"I already knew you were hurting."

He continued as if he didn't hear her. "The harder I worked, the more I realized what I said earlier. The more I realized you're Fred."

"What?" Now she knew she had to be dreaming because none of this made sense.

He sniffed, and it sounded suspiciously like a chuckle. "You're not a bag of bolts like the truck, but he's been around for a long time. Your granddaddy loved him. So did you. Bob has treated him right too. Wasn't a lot of work to prettying him up. But you weren't treated right. You had no idea

idea how to lay out any kind of love because your dad never put any work into loving you. Frankly, the way I acted then . . . I'd have run, too, if I were you." He ran his hand through his hair and gripped the back of his neck. "It wasn't my best day."

"Mine, either."

"If I know you, and I think I do, you've hurt over this for a long time. Well, I'm just beginning. It's going to take some time to get over the shock, but it's time you stopped carrying it by yourself. And I'll be honest. I don't think I'm capable of dealing with this on my own."

The ringing in her ears wouldn't let her comprehend the words until he stepped down from the porch and was standing in front of her, closer than she thought he'd ever be again.

"Your grandmother's best friend, she doesn't quit. She came to see me a couple of days ago."

"Marnie?" What in the world was she thinking, digging her nose where it didn't belong? She might not be Jemma's sister, but she definitely behaved like the same blood coursed through their veins.

"Yeah. She reminded me about what it means to love somebody. And what it means to forgive. Told me about the letter you never got." Justin tucked a stray hair behind Taryn's ear. "Fact of the matter is, McKenna, I do love you. I'm pretty sure I never stopped. But you're going to have to forgive me for being an impulsive, angry kid who said some pretty harsh things to you when you were hurting. If I hadn't . . ." His eyes finally landed on hers. "Who knows what would have been different today?"

"You were going to ask me to marry you?"

He nodded.

"At eighteen."

Another nod. "And here's the other thing."

Taryn arched an eyebrow, out of words. He was standing too close, stealing all of her air and revving her heartbeat. If this was a dream, she wanted to keep on having it.

"I'm going to ask you again at thirty."

Her whole face went slack. Her chin must have dropped to her knees.

"Way I figure it, God's got a sense of humor." He stepped out of her line of sight and reached into the back of the truck, then came back, a large box between them.

Taryn didn't have to open it to know what it was. "The quilt."

"Jemma started it for us and hid it away, only you found it just in time for me to act all girly and sew it with you." His grin slipped. "I don't believe in coincidence." He slid the box over her head onto the roof of the truck. "I knew once I moved back, we'd see each other. When Jemma called, it seemed like maybe the time was right. God was thinking we needed more than me fixing a roof, I guess, so He brought together a leaky roof, two quilts, and my amazing talent with a needle."

More than anything, Taryn wanted to sink into him, let him wrap his arms around her, and tell him she was his forever. But she couldn't. It wouldn't be fair. Taryn lay her palms on his chest, warm through the thick, coarse black of his coat. "I can't marry you."

"I didn't ask. Yet. There's a lot for both of us to work through. I'm going to hang onto the quilt until you're ready for it. Deal?" He smiled and planted a kiss on her forehead. "My first thought is we have a trip to take to Texas soon. Together. There's someone we both need to meet."

He understood. Taryn gripped his biceps like she'd spin off the planet if she let go. And he was willing to wait for her to get it straight. "Know what, Callahan?"

A full-blown grin erupted. "What, McKenna?"

"I'm pretty sure I love you too."

He finally, blessedly, wrapped his arms around her and pulled her close, warming her from the inside out. "Then what more could I want for Christmas?"

"Legos."

"What?" The word cracked on a laugh.

"I bought you Legos."

"Then my life is complete." All trace of laughter gone, he closed the space between them, brushed a quick kiss, then came in for one longer, deeper, full of promise, and forgiveness and love, like Taryn had never been offered before.

She accepted. Because there really was such a thing as Christmas "magic," where God's hand could lead you to a place where all your dreams came true.

Group Discussion Guide

1. Family plays a central role in Taryn's life, and her father and grandmother in particular play major—if opposite—roles. Describe someone in your family who had a profound influence on your life.

2. Have you, like Taryn, ever kept a secret you shouldn't have kept? How did it affect your emotions? Your relationship with the person you kept the secret from? Your relationship with God?

3. The McKennas have a tradition of giving each new bride a quilt, symbolically linking the generations. Describe a tradition your family has or discuss one that you would like to start.

4. When Taryn is talking to her student, she says, "Real love is freely given, not taken away because you don't do what someone wants." Read 1 Peter 4:8. How does it apply to what Taryn says?

5. Tell about a time when someone forgave you for something that you thought was "unforgivable." Is there someone you need to forgive?

6. Toward the end of the novel, Taryn prays, "*Lord, I did all of the right things for all of the wrong reasons.*" Has there ever been a time when you did the right thing, but your motives were wrong? What happened in the end? What does James 4:3 say about our motives?

7. On Christmas morning, Taryn determines to set aside everything and make Christmas about her relationship

with Christ. This Christmas, what can you do to place Christ at the center of the season?

8. Sometimes the hardest thing to do is forgive ourselves. Is there something in your past that you find yourself continually going to God to ask for forgiveness for? God's forgiven you, is it possible you haven't forgiven yourself?

9. How does Taryn's life exemplify 2 Corinthians 5:17? How does this verse apply to your life?

10. How do Justin's actions in the final chapter express 1 Corinthians 13:7?

Want to learn more about author
Jodie Bailey and check out other great
fiction from Abingdon Press?

Check out
www.AbingdonFiction.com
to read interviews with your favorite authors, find tips
for starting a reading group, and stay posted on what
new titles are on the horizon.

You can also check out all of the Quilts of Love series at
www.quiltsoflovebooks.com

Be sure to visit Jodie online!

www.jodiebailey.com

We hope that you enjoyed Jodie Bailey's *Quilted by Christmas*, and that you will check out other Quilts of Love books. The next one in the series is Laura V. Hilton and Cindy Loven's *Swept Away*. Here's a sample chapter.

———

1

Sara Jane Morgan gasped for breath, scanning the crowded pathways. Everyone showed up for the Heritage Festival, which was good for the artists and vendors, but bad for her. Especially considering . . .

No. She couldn't voice her concerns. At least not yet. But losing a loved one in this mob would cause anyone to panic. This was why mothers kept their toddlers locked securely in strollers and older children attached to harnesses with straps.

But one couldn't exactly fasten a grandmother to a leash. And Sara Jane, being a grown woman, shouldn't be having a panic attack.

She pulled in a shaking breath and forced herself to calm down. She could handle this. Stepping to the side of the paved walkway, she let a woman pushing a double stroller pass, then a man driving a motorized wheelchair. She feigned interest in the open-air tent beside her. A display of corncob dolls. People still made them?

Well, this was the Appalachians. There were tourists here from all over the country who expected to find mountain handcrafts for sale.

She merged into the crowd and peeked into the next tent, making sure to get a look at the people inside. This one show-cased CDs and DVDs by Appalachian musicians—or rather, one particular group. Pretending to shop while scanning the customers, she lifted a case off the rack by the entrance and looked at the picture. Banjos, played by guys in overalls. She put it back.

Another booth held pocketknives, hunting, fishing, and utility knives. Grandma wouldn't be here. Mostly men any-way. She moved on.

The tent next to it held screen-printed T-shirts . . .

Panic filled her again. Grandma had wandered farther than she expected. How long had she been missing before Sara Jane realized she'd gotten lost? She pushed her way past a few peo-ple holding a conversation in the middle of the sidewalk. She caught a glimpse of a uniformed Boy Scout. Weren't they sup-posed to help people? He disappeared into the throng before she caught up to him.

Sara Jane went on to the next display. Oh. Wow. Brightly colored quilts. This was where she would have expected to find Grandma. She loved to quilt and belonged to the Christian Women's group at church. But Grandma wasn't with the women oohing and ahhing over the quilts.

Maybe. A gray-haired woman stood off to the back, head bowed as she studied the stitching. No, she wasn't Grandma. Her hair was a different cut, and she wore a green T-shirt and a blue jean skirt. Sara Jane would come back and check this tent again later, in case Grandma made her way here.

The next tent was completely enclosed, the canvas doors tied open with twine. Sara Jane poked her head in, ready to rush on. The tent was void of people except for two, a man and Grandma.

Expelling a breath she hadn't realized she held, Sara Jane grasped the edge of the tent door and forced herself to look around.

Grandma was in here. With brooms. Whoever knew there were so many ways to make a broom?

The man behind the table looked as bushy as his wares. His shaggy brown beard hung down to his collar, and a rumpled button-up shirt draped over his blue jeans. His hair was almost as long as his beard. He looked up as she entered. His eyes reminded her of dark chocolate.

Grandma stood beside the scruffy-looking man, holding a piece of paper, saying words Sara Jane couldn't catch due to the sudden rush of blood in her ears. She turned. "Oh, there you are, Sara Jane. I hired Andrew to do some odd jobs around my house since I'm thinking of selling. Doesn't he have the cutest business card?" She held out the card stock.

Sara Jane took it and gave it a cursory glance. *Starving artist/ pay the bills handyman* in bold, colorful print topped the card. Andrew Stevenson. Followed by a phone number and a picture of a bright red tool box. She handed it back to Grandma. "Adorable."

The adjective didn't apply to the owner of the card.

"Grandma, don't you think you'd rather hire someone we actually know to do the repairs?"

⸻⸱⸻

"Sara Jane! I raised you to treat people better."

Drew Stevenson tried to control his grin as the older woman tore into the younger one.

Rude or not, he couldn't tear his gaze away from Sara Jane. She was . . . stunning. But so not his type. A woman like her would never look twice at a man like him. Not as if he'd want her to.

She had long dark hair, the color of espresso coffee. He couldn't see her eyes, hidden behind sunglasses, but he imagined they'd be brown, like her hair. Or maybe hazel. She wore tailored jeans, undoubtedly designer, the type with a permanent crease up the front middle of the leg. A fitted blouse in a shade of a pinkish-orange reminded him of peaches. The top two or three buttons were unhooked, giving a tantalizing glimpse of . . .

He glanced away. He had no right to look. Her husband . . . he scanned her hand. Not married. Her boyfriend wouldn't appreciate another man ogling his girl.

Her gaze skittered over his brooms with a dismissive look, the same one she'd bestowed upon him. As if he weren't worthy of consideration—either as a broom maker or a man. His passion and art deserved some appreciation. Irritation ate at him. His hand tightened around the handle of the broom closest to him.

"Sorry, Grandma, and you, too, Mr. uh . . . sir, but I don't think . . ."

He ranked so low on her importance scale she didn't remember his name. Oh. That hurt. He clenched his jaw. He refused to think of the time he asked a woman out, and she laughed in his face, as if he'd been telling a joke.

The older woman stiffened. "I don't care what you think. It's my decision, Sara Jane. My house. And my right to . . ."

Drew straightened his spine and turned away from them, rearranging a display as he tried not to listen to the animated conversation. It wasn't too hard when other people drifted into the tent.

"Oooh, look at these brooms! Isn't this a cute little one? What's it used for?"

He looked at the middle-aged woman in front of him. "It's called a turkey wing broom. It's used for brushing off counter tops and tables or other surfaces."

"It's so cute. How much do you charge for it? Do you do custom orders? I like pink and try to keep everything as pink as possible around my house."

He worked his mouth a second before he found his voice. "Pink. Yes, ma'am, I do custom orders." But pink? "It'd be slightly more expensive, though."

"Oh, it's okay." The woman whipped a pink cell phone out of her pocket. "Let me take a picture of you with this broom. You look like a real mountain man."

<hr />

Sara Jane's mouth dried even as tears burned her eyes. Grandma intended to sell her house? Since when? She'd never mentioned it in all the conversations they'd had recently.

Putting the Appalachian-style log cabin Grandpa had built Grandma as a new bride aside, how could Grandma think of hiring someone who looked like this man? Didn't he own a razor? He looked as if he came straight out of the wilderness, like a John the Baptist wannabe. Maybe he ate locusts and honey.

Her stomach clenched. By the looks of him, he could be a mass murderer, with the beard to keep people from recognizing his picture on the most wanted list. She peered at him again. He looked familiar. He'd probably been on a recent episode of *America's Most Wanted*.

He did make nice-looking brooms, assuming he'd actually done the work, but it didn't matter in the least. She couldn't allow Grandma to hire him.

Besides, Grandma kept hiring incompetent people, like the last one Sara Jane discovered stuffing sterling silver candleholders in his toolbox.

Maybe if she changed the subject . . . Sara Jane gently took her grandmother by the elbow and steered her farther away from the table. "You scared me out of my skin, taking off like that. What were you thinking?"

Grandma frowned and shook her head. "I didn't take off. You were the one who wasn't paying attention. You obviously didn't hear me when I said I wanted to see what else was out there. Not everyone is interested in looking at books about Daniel Boone and forts and what types of Indians were native to these hills."

Okay, that'd been about the time Grandma had gone missing.

"I didn't know you were thinking of selling your house. We'll discuss it later. If you need a handyman, why don't you hire your nice neighbor, Charlie Jones, to work on the house for you? We don't know this man."

Grandma made an unfeminine snort and rolled her eyes. "I don't need a babysitter. Have you ever considered you're smothering me?"

Sara Jane gasped. Smothering? How could Grandma think she was?

"Besides, Charlie Jones can't work on my house. He died a year ago." Grandma folded her arms and stared Sara Jane down.

Sara Jane tried hard not to sigh. Her handy excuse to get Grandma away from the John the Baptist impersonator disappeared and made her look foolish in the process. And since when did Grandma get so argumentative? It had to be something to do with old age. She'd read something about it in a magazine article somewhere.

"Grandma . . ."

"Sara Jane, I like this young man and I intend to hire him. It's my house and my decision. And that's final." Grandma punctuated it with a decisive nod. "He'll be there Monday at eight."